Tales from the
WITCH'S COTTAGE

Hanna Karlzon

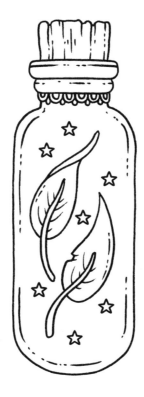

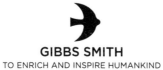

GIBBS SMITH
TO ENRICH AND INSPIRE HUMANKIND

25 24 23   5 4 3

Tales from the Witch's Cottage Coloring Book
Illustrations © 2022 Hanna Karlzon

Original title: *Berättelser från häxans stuga*

Copyright © Hanna Karlzon och Tukan förlag 2022
Illustrations and design: Hanna Karlzon
www.hannakarlzon.com

First published by Tukan förlag 2021
Örlogsvägen 15
426 71 Västra Frölunda
Sweden
www.tukanforlag.se

English edition copyright © 2022 Gibbs Smith Publisher, USA.

Gibbs Smith
P.O. Box 667
Layton, Utah 84041

1.800.835.4993 orders
www.gibbs-smith.com

ISBN: 978-1-4236-6165-8

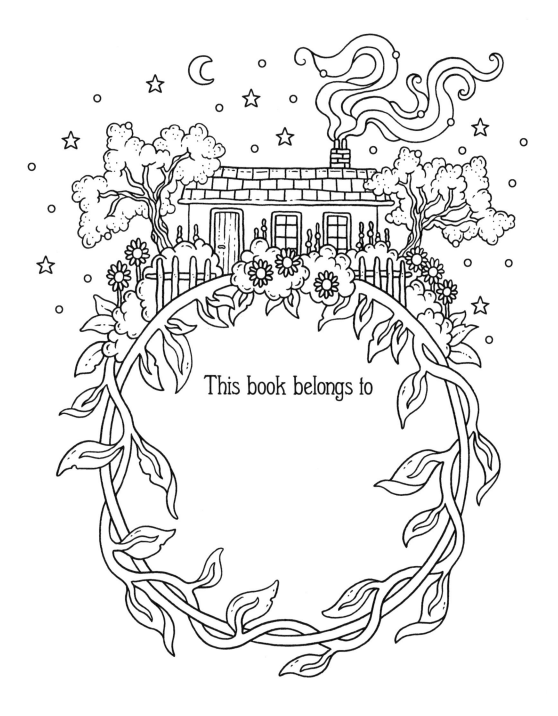

This book belongs to

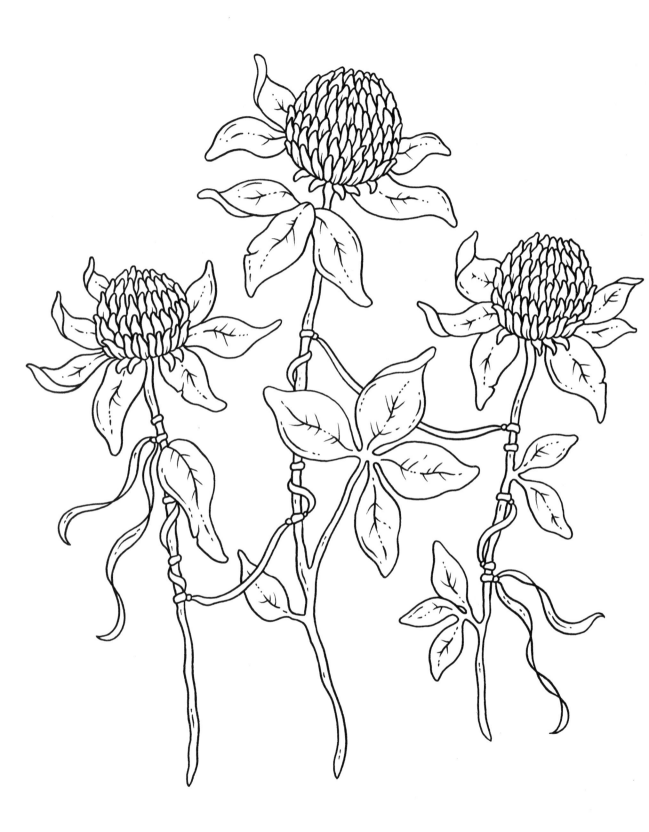

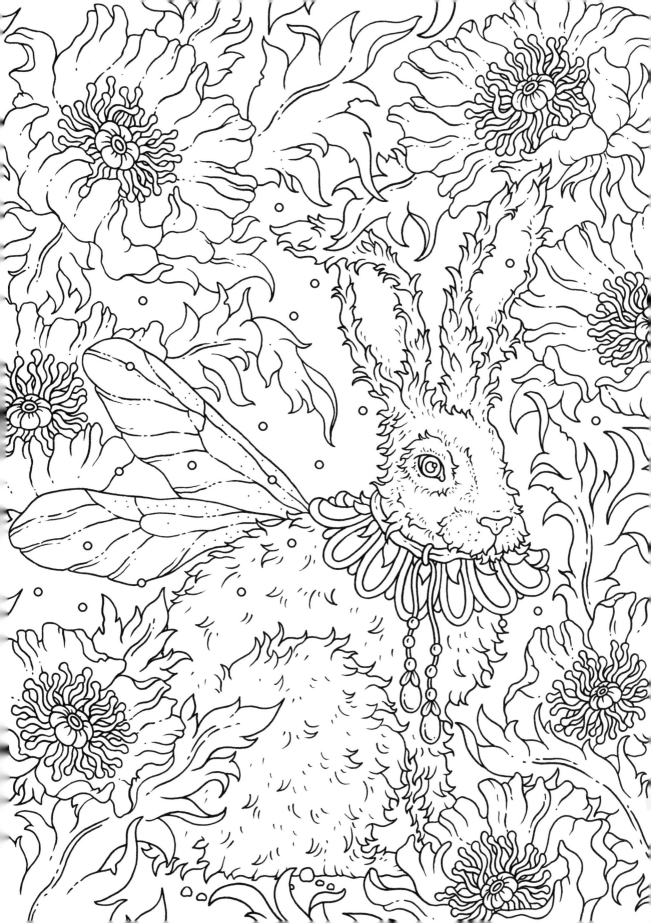

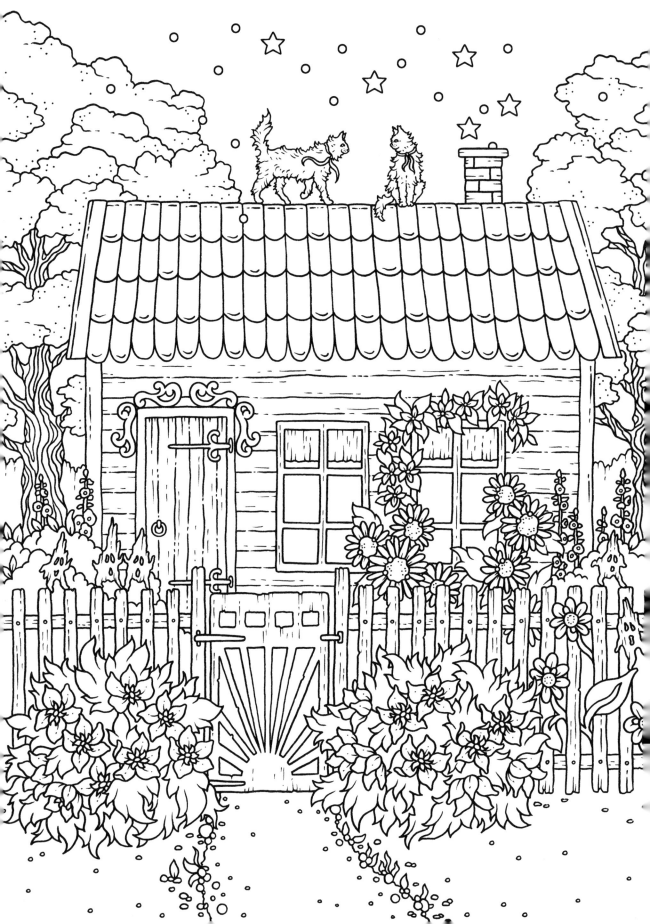

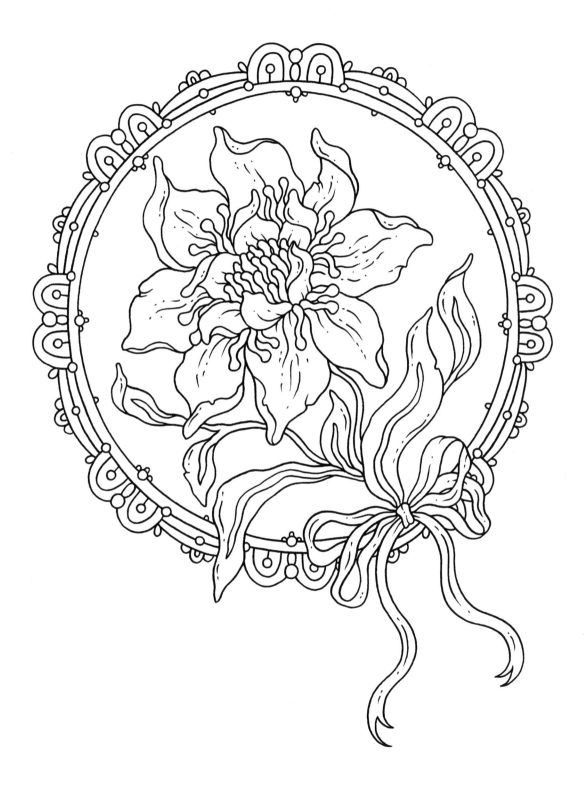

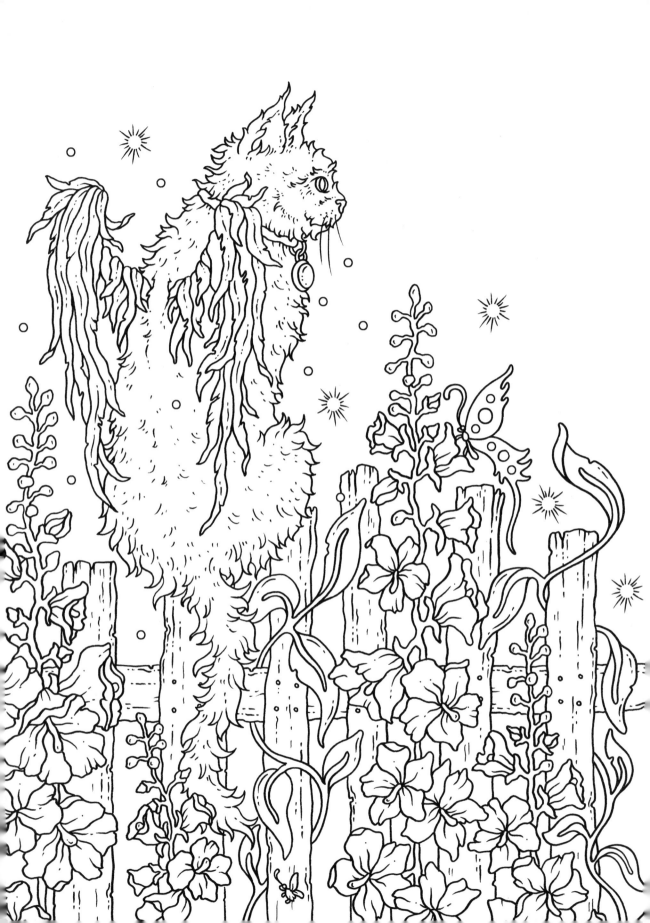

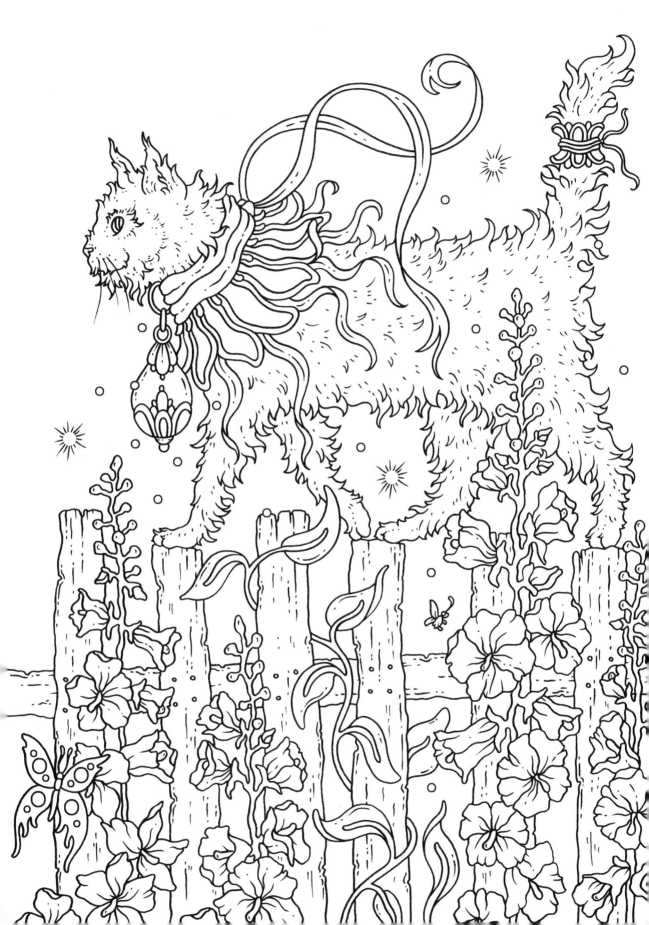

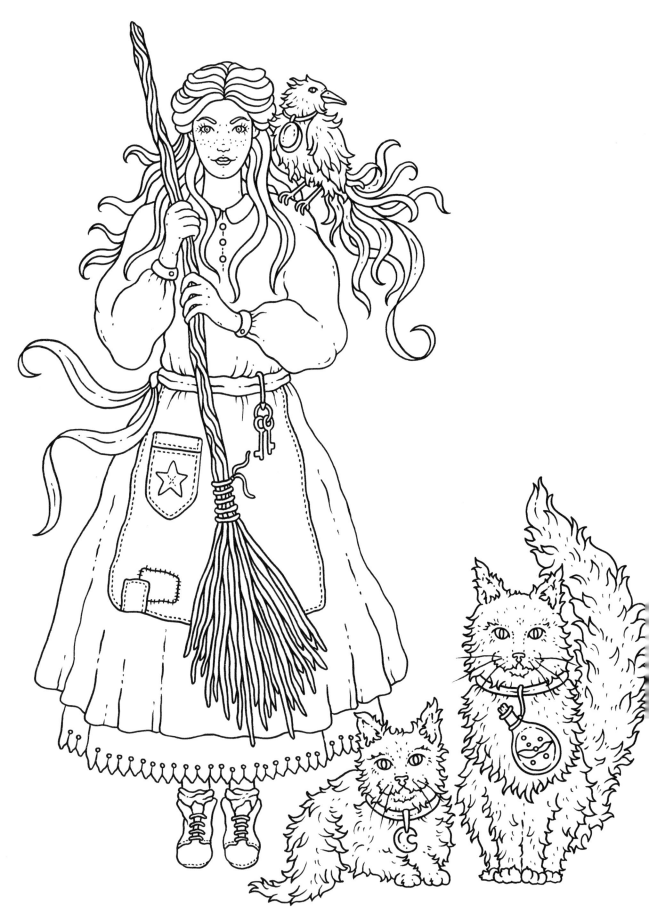

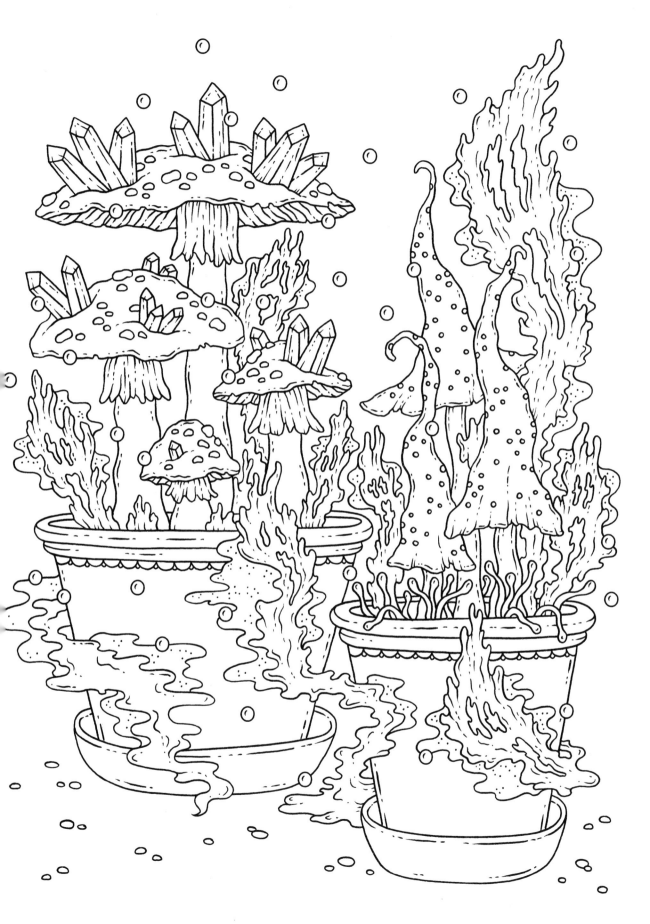

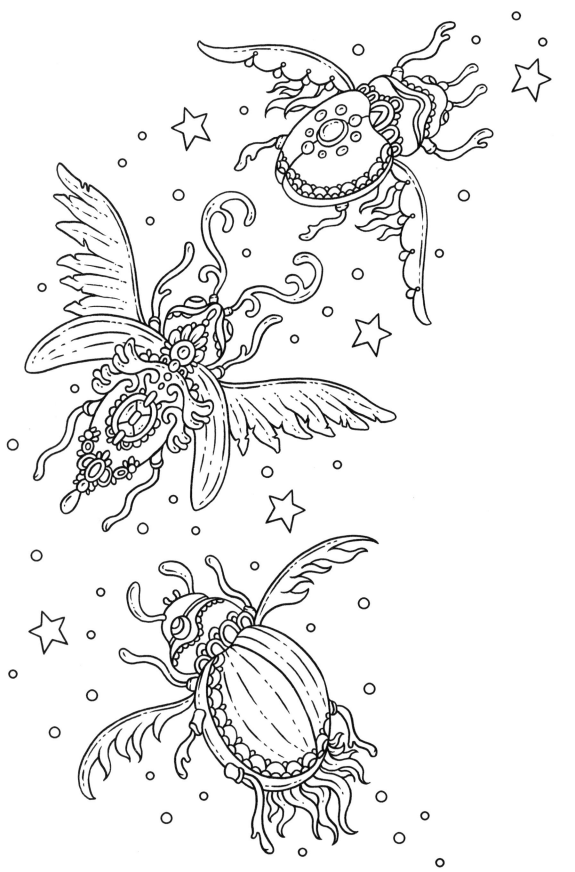

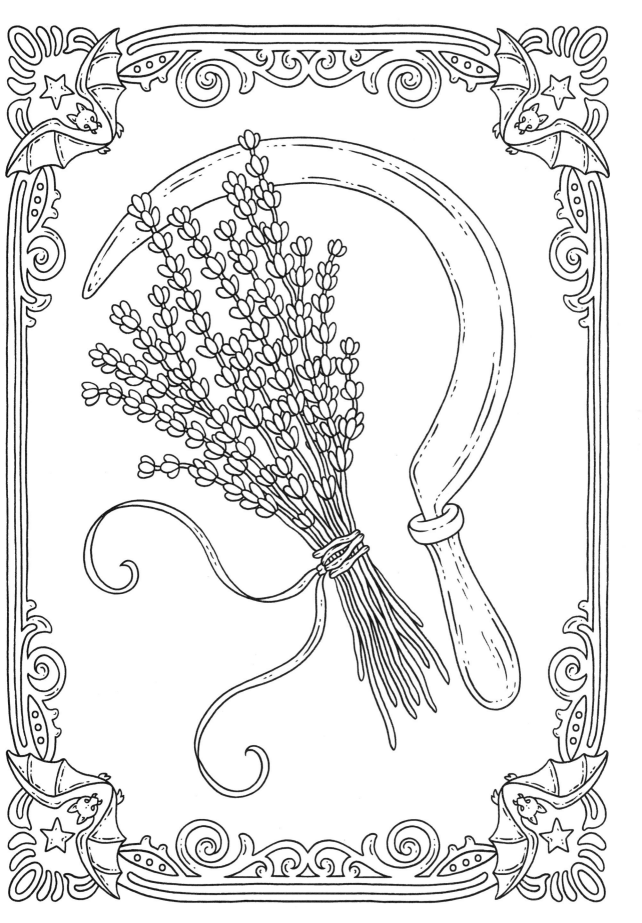

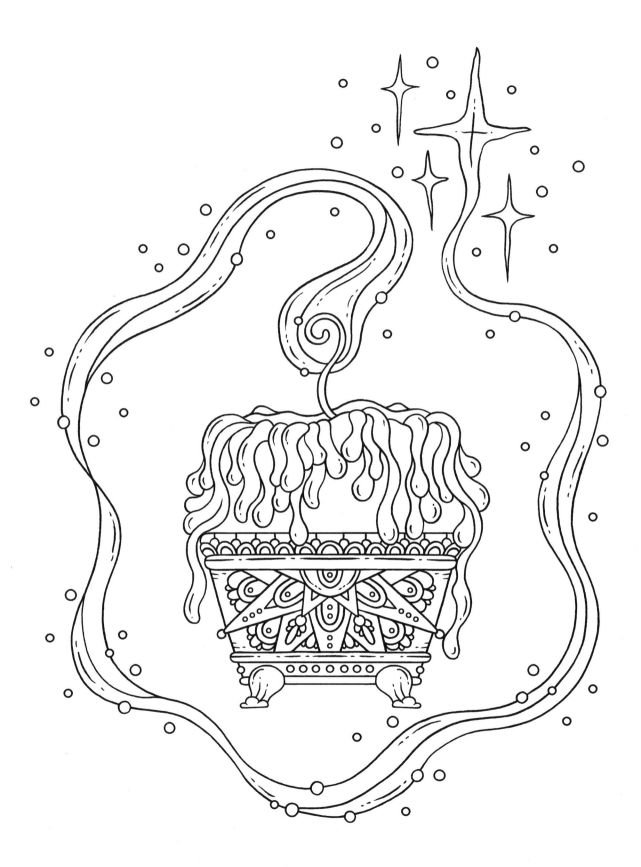

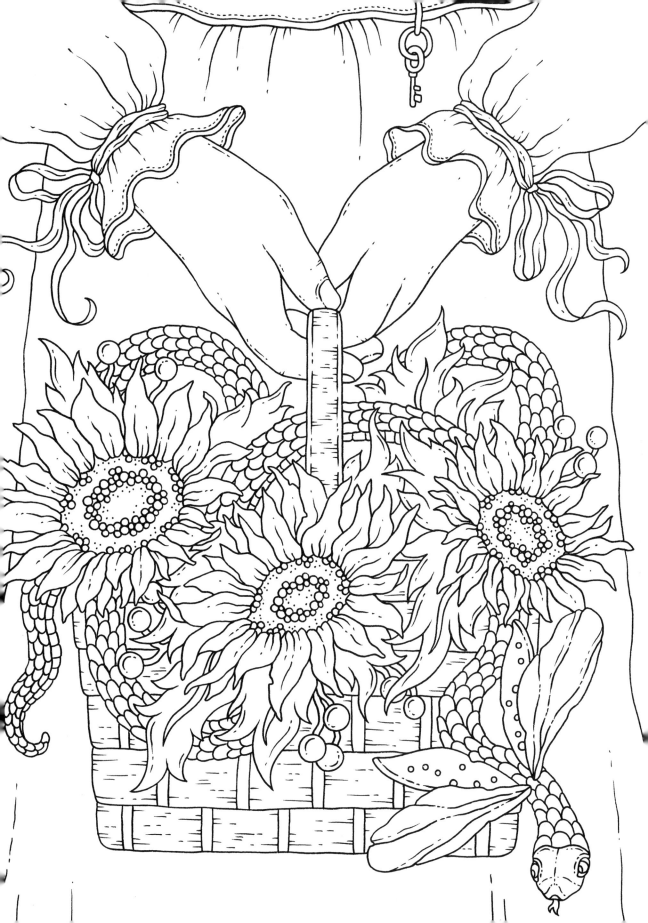

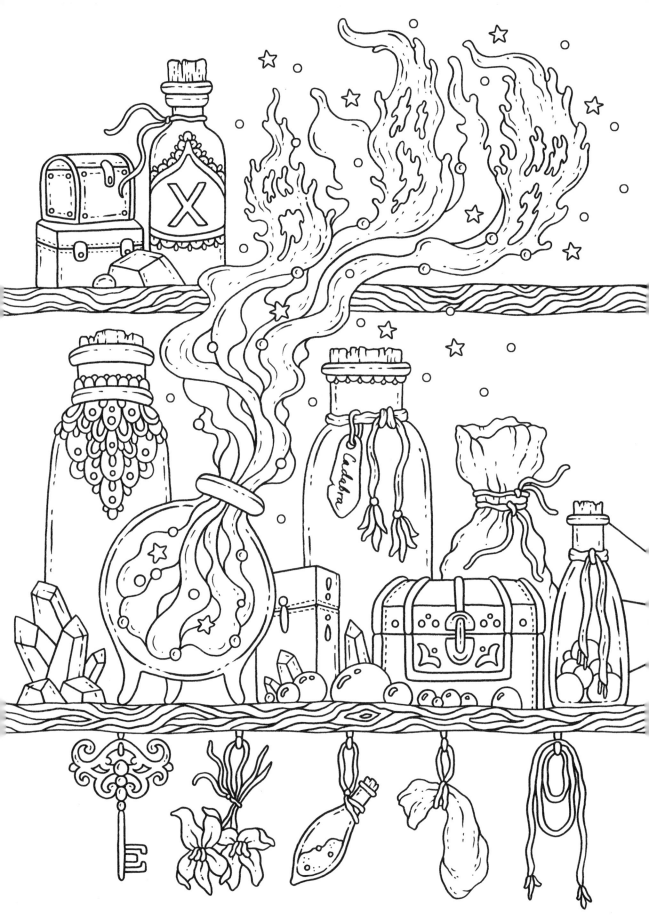

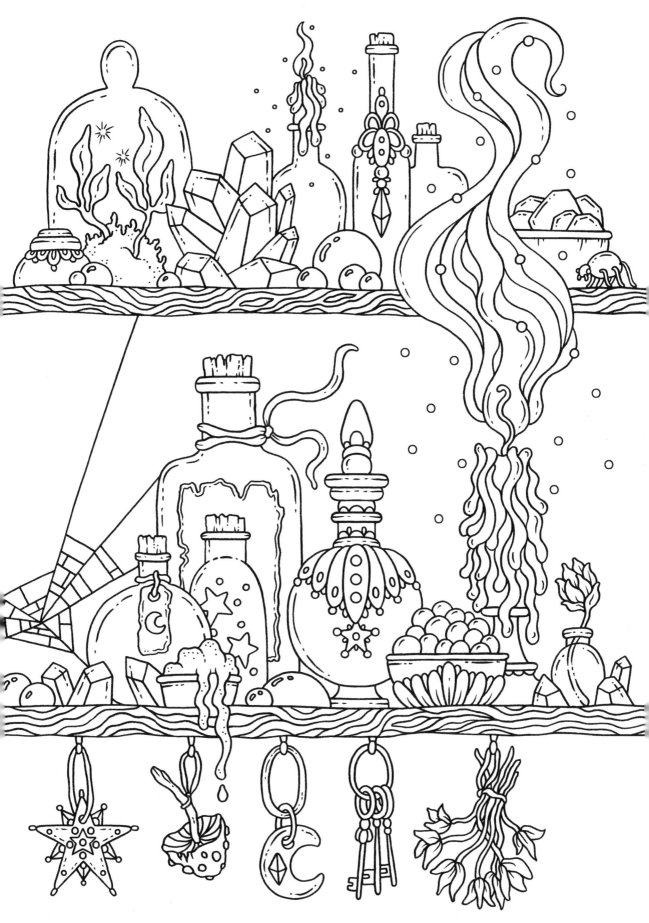

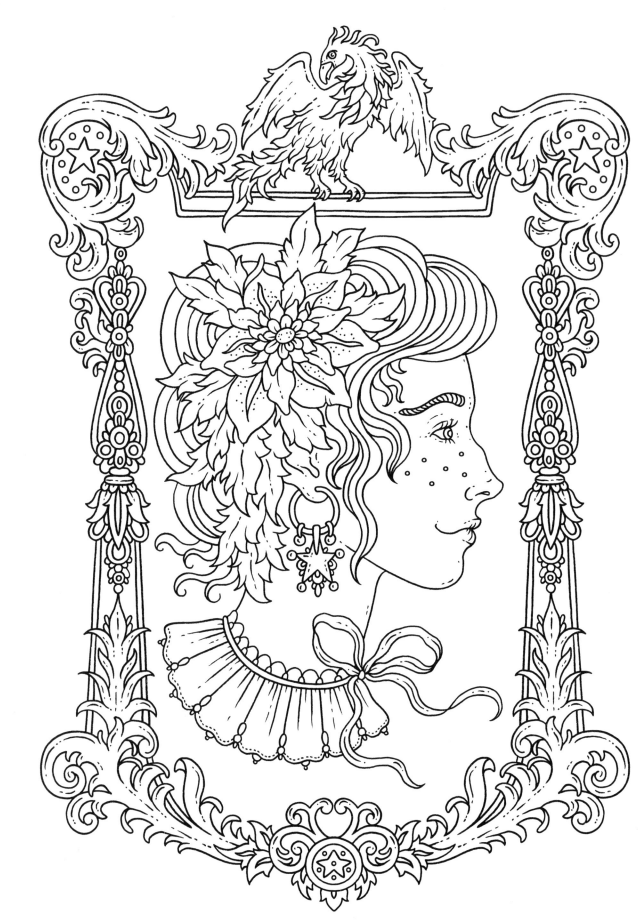

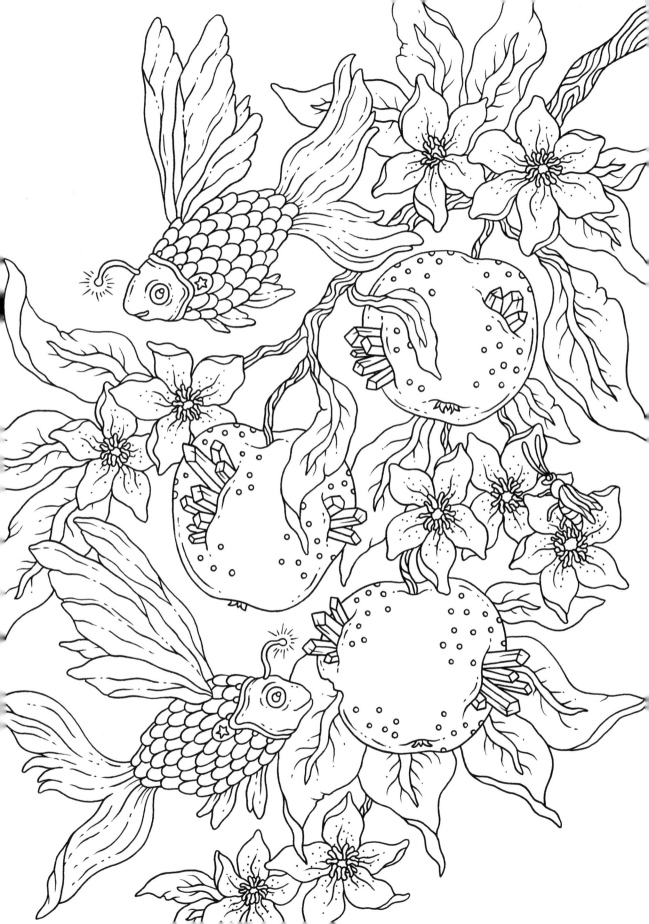

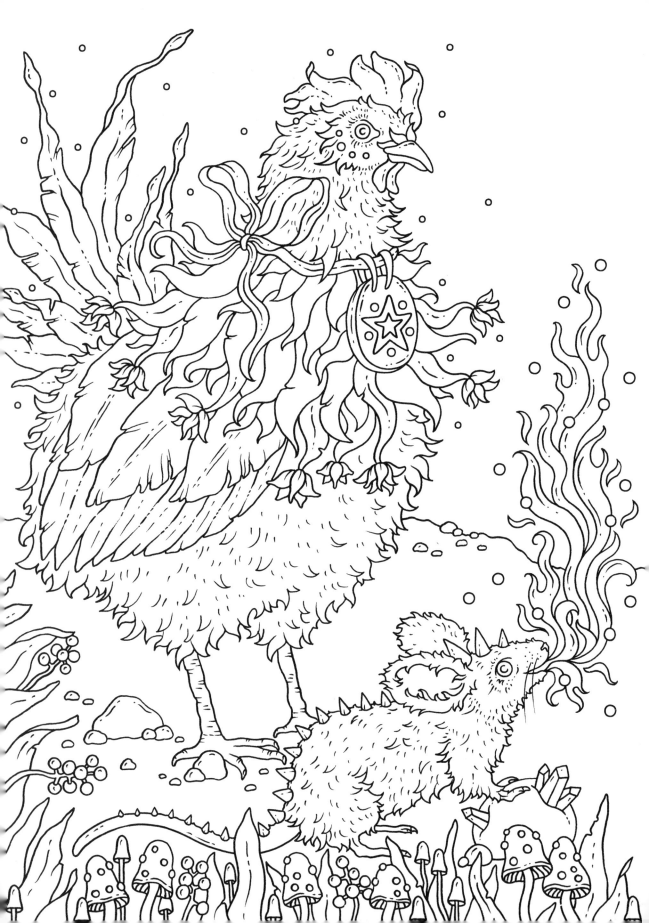

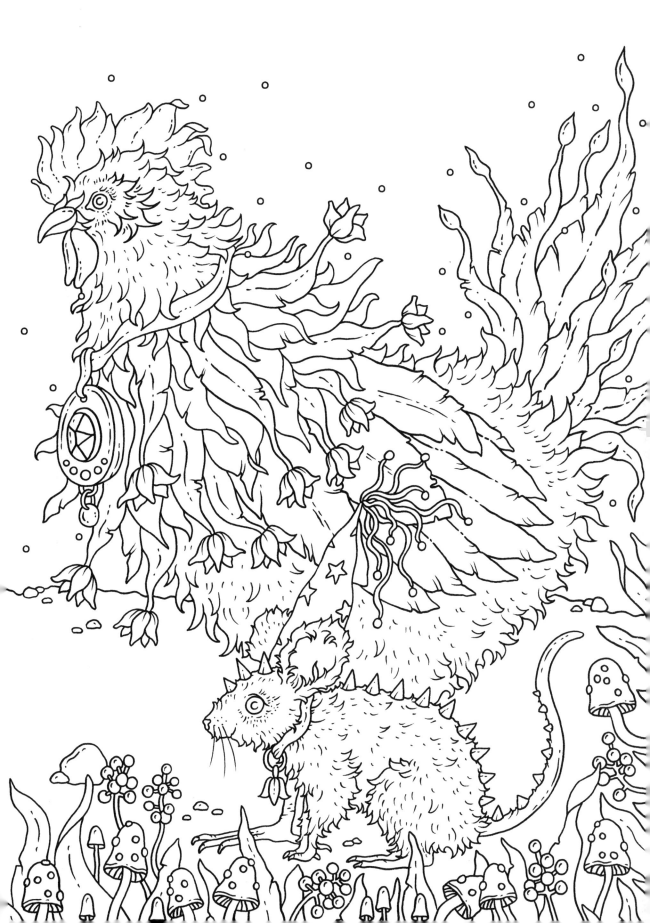

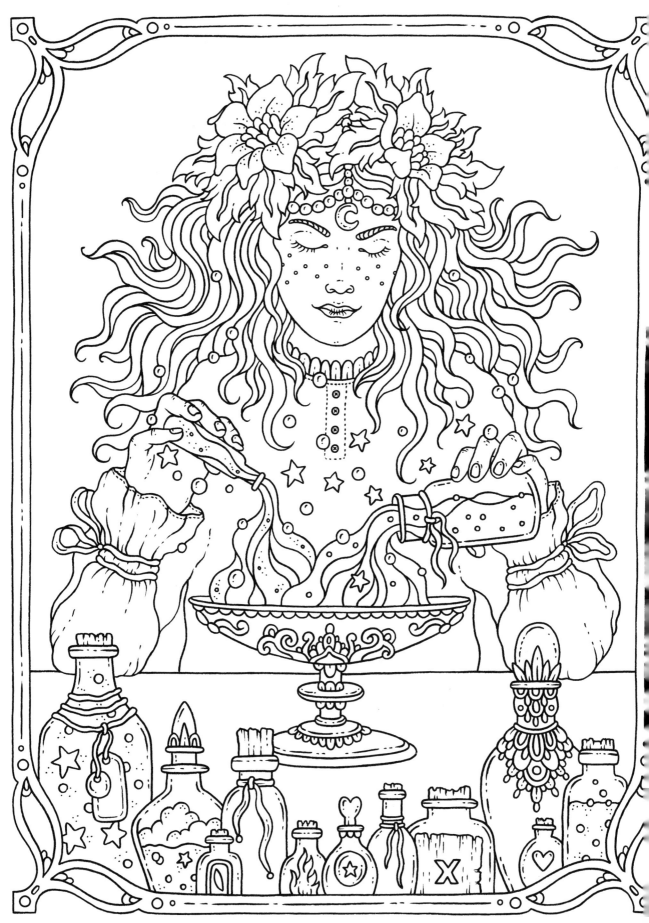

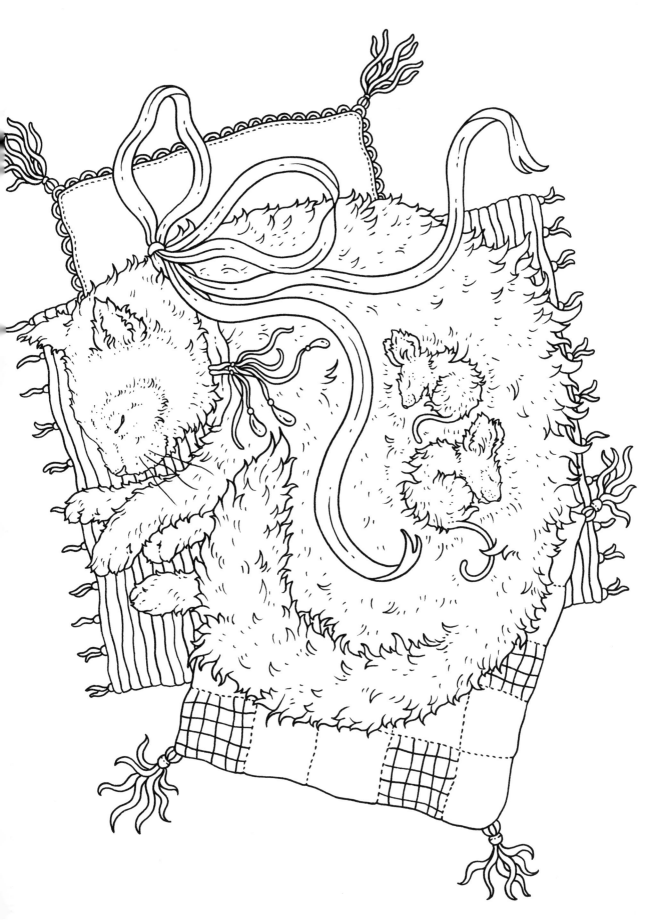

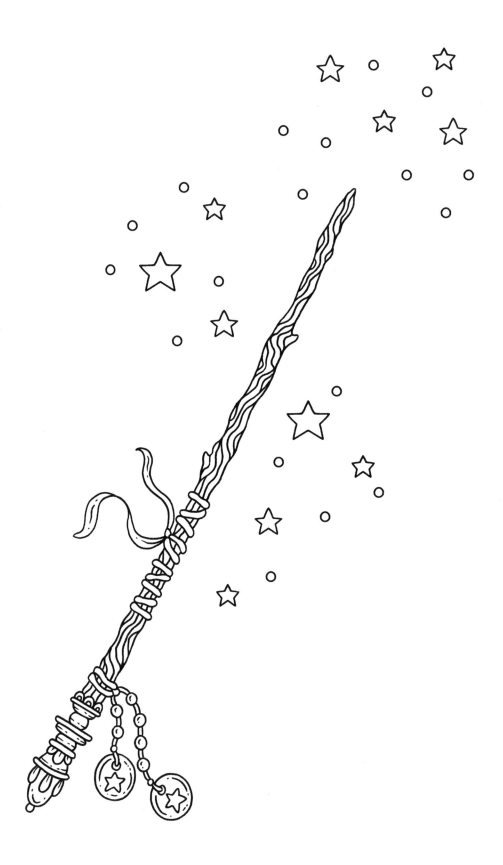

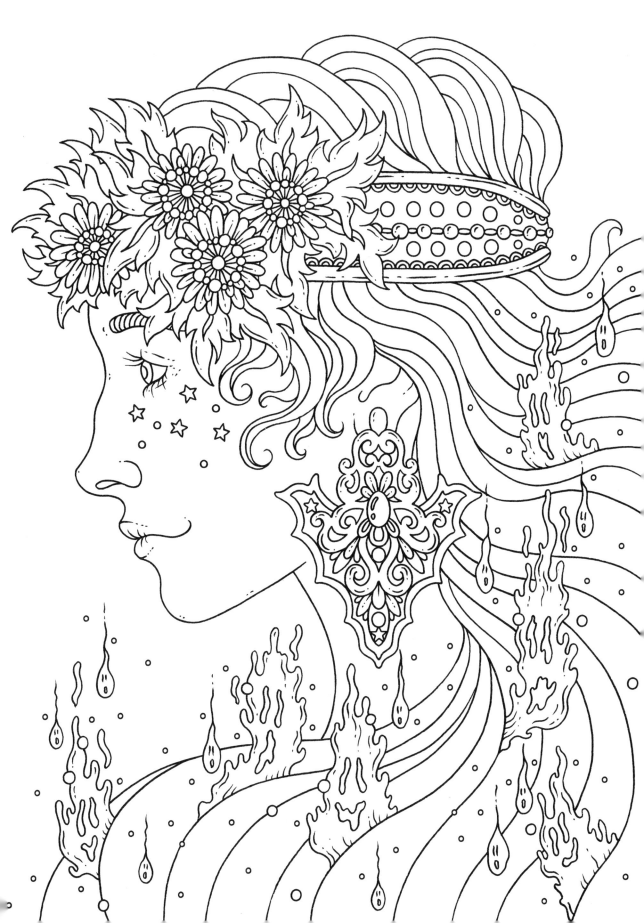

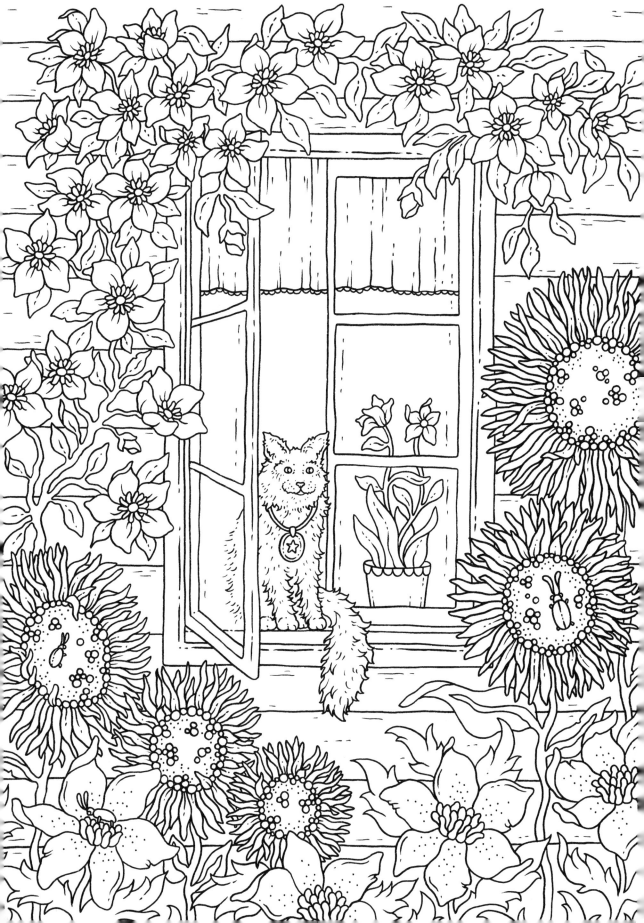

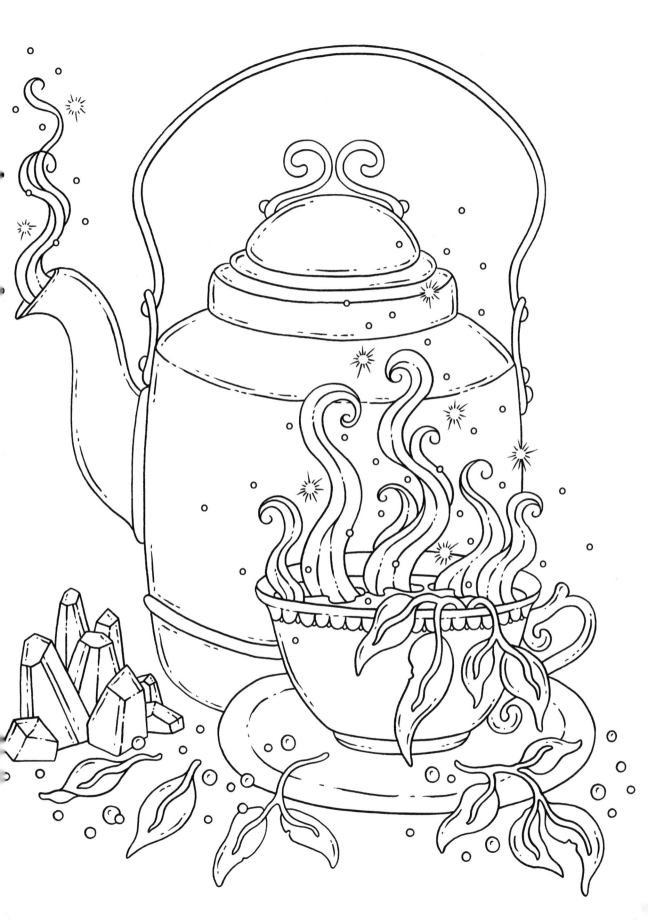

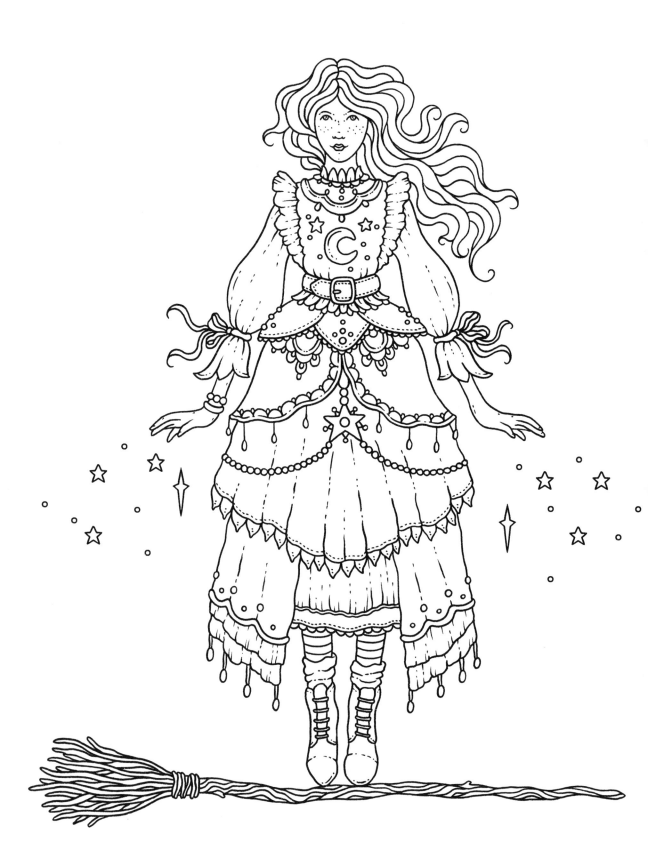

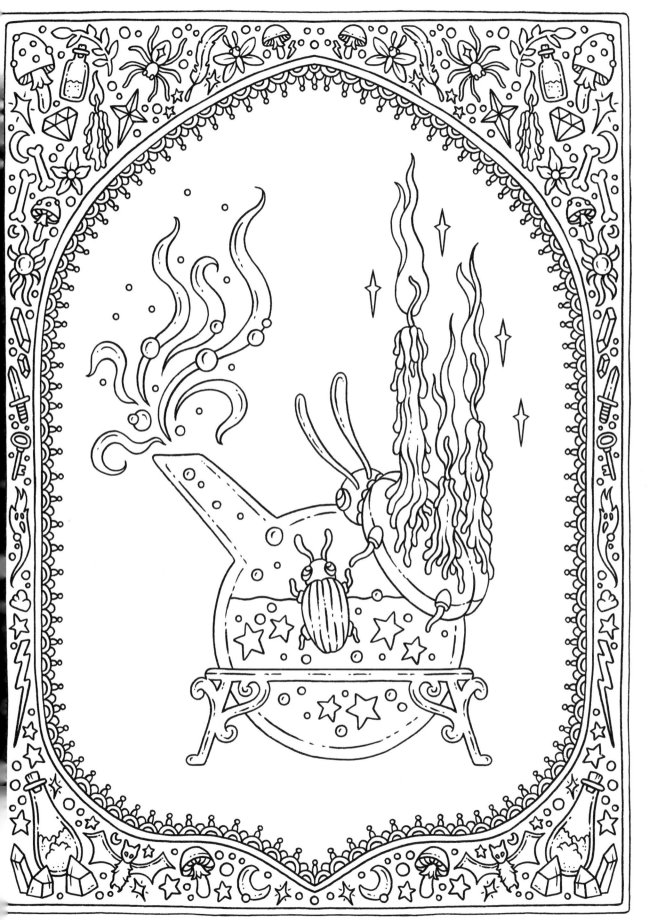

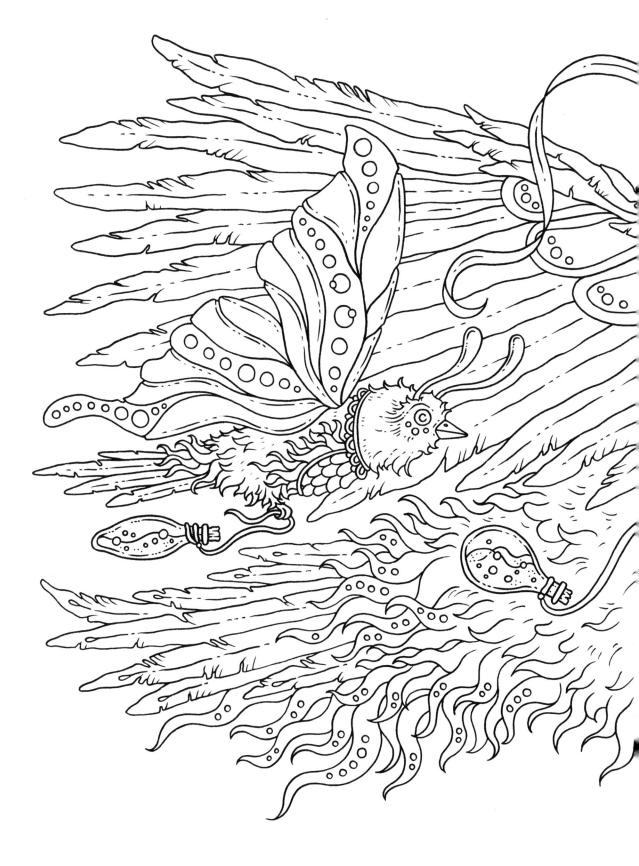

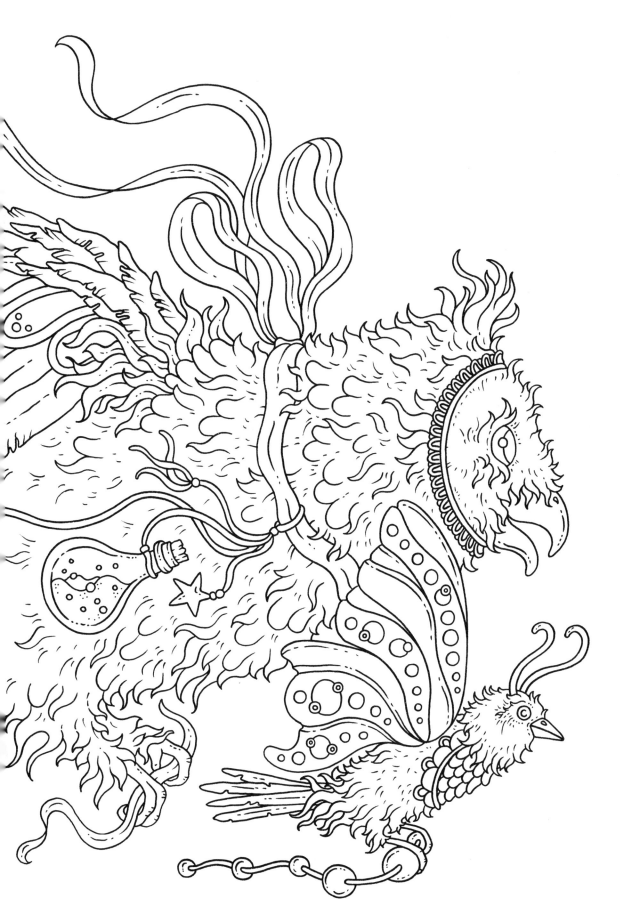

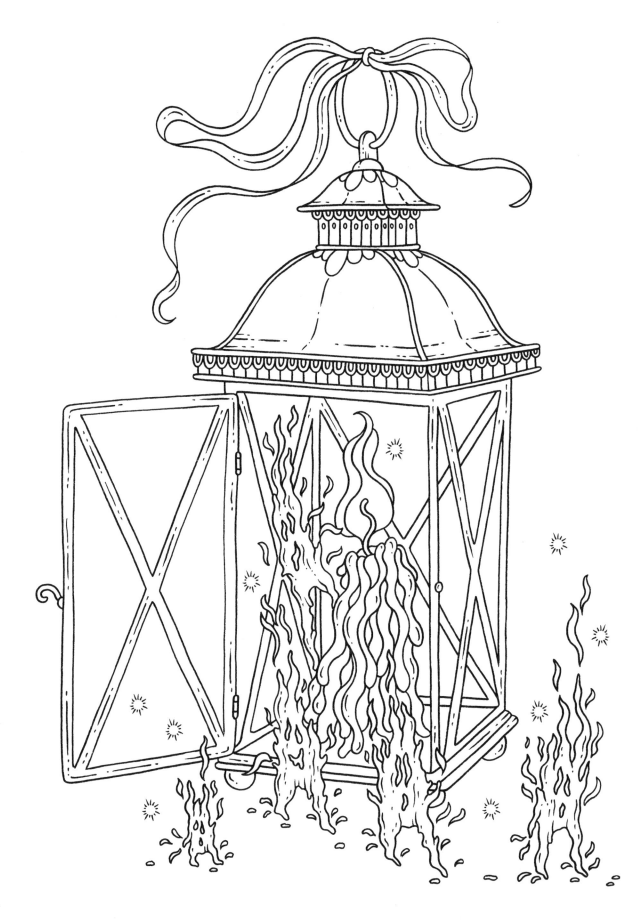

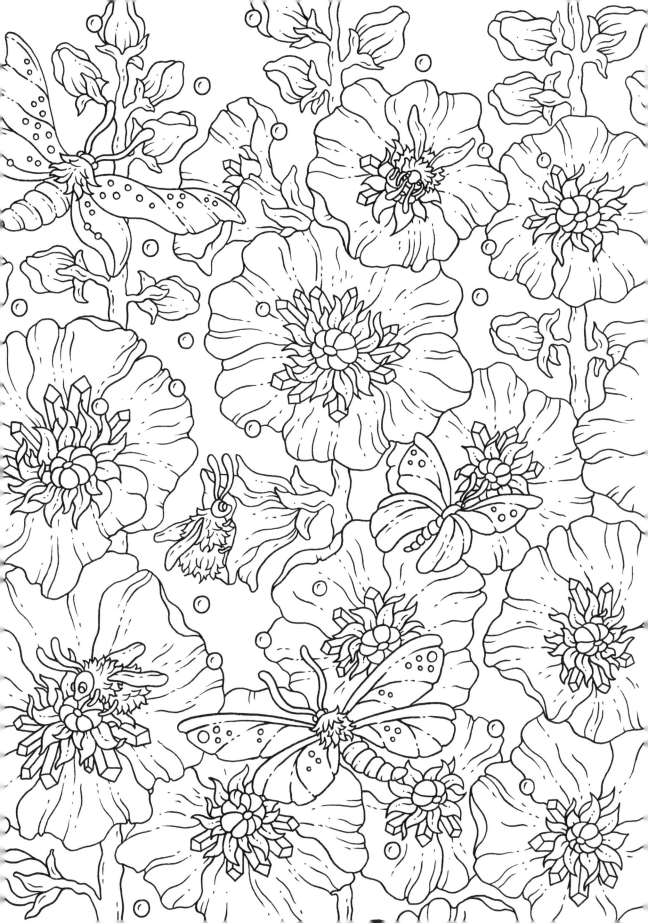

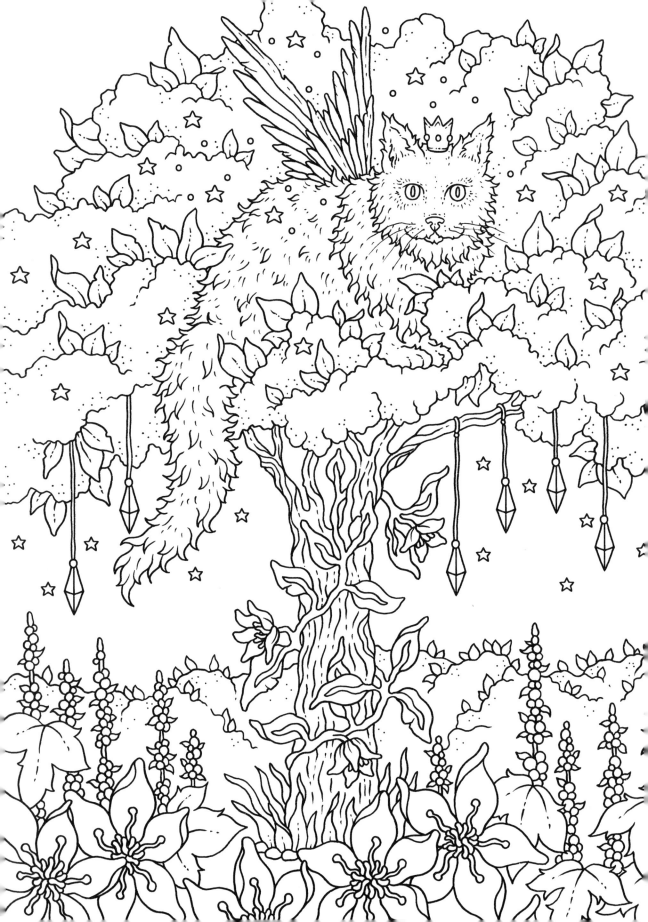

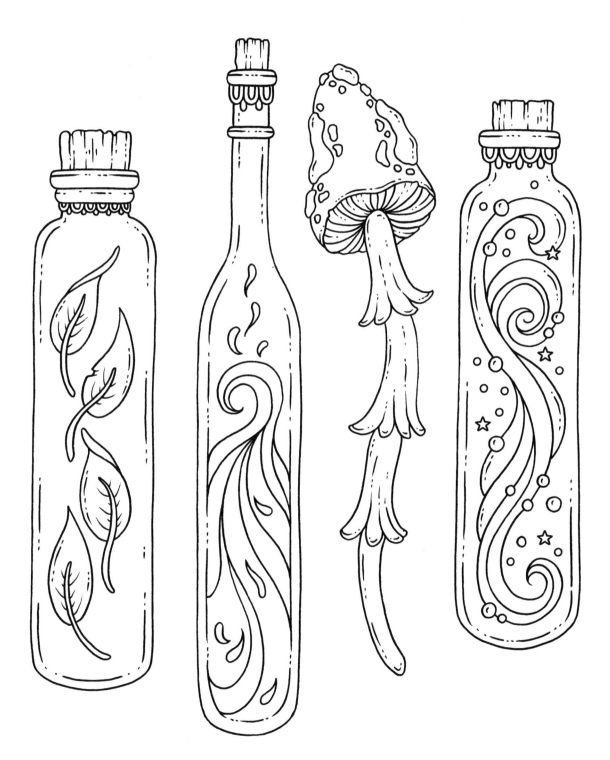

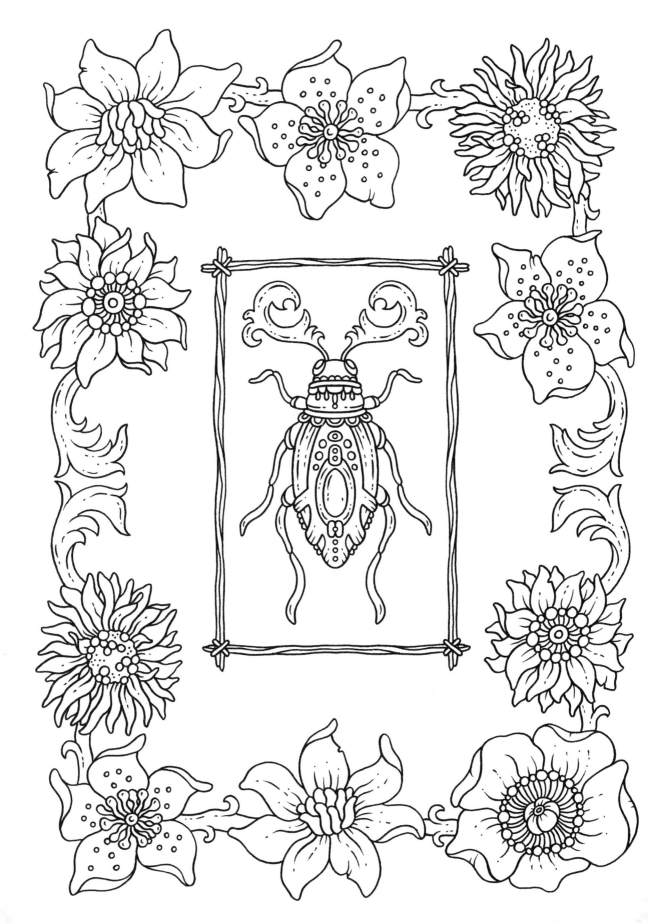

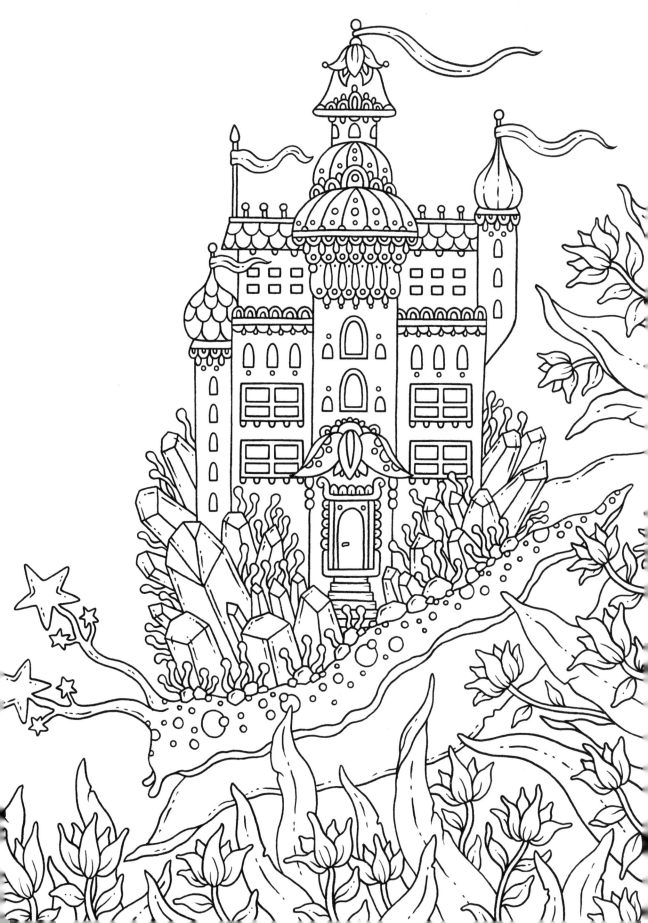

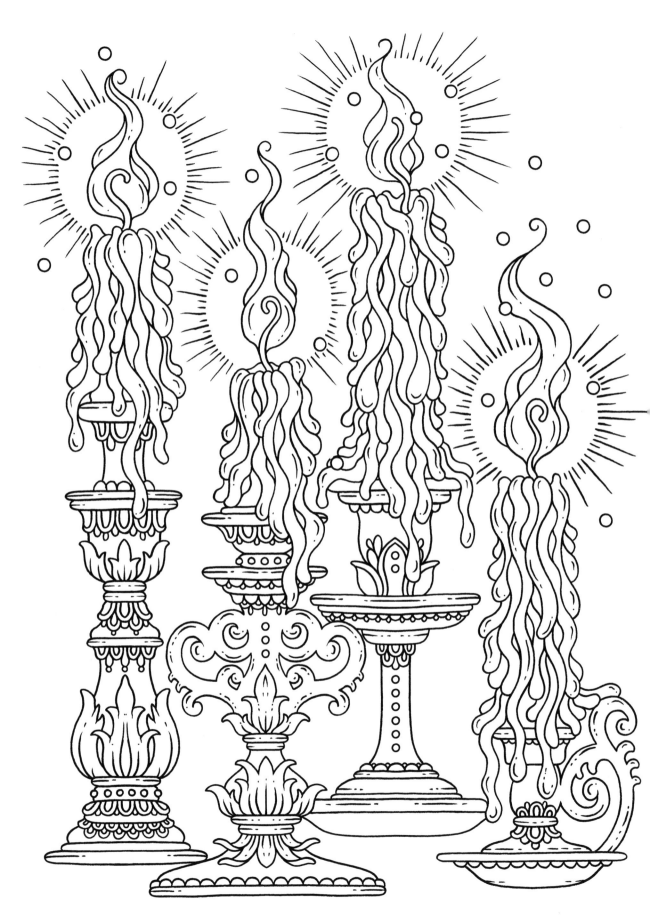

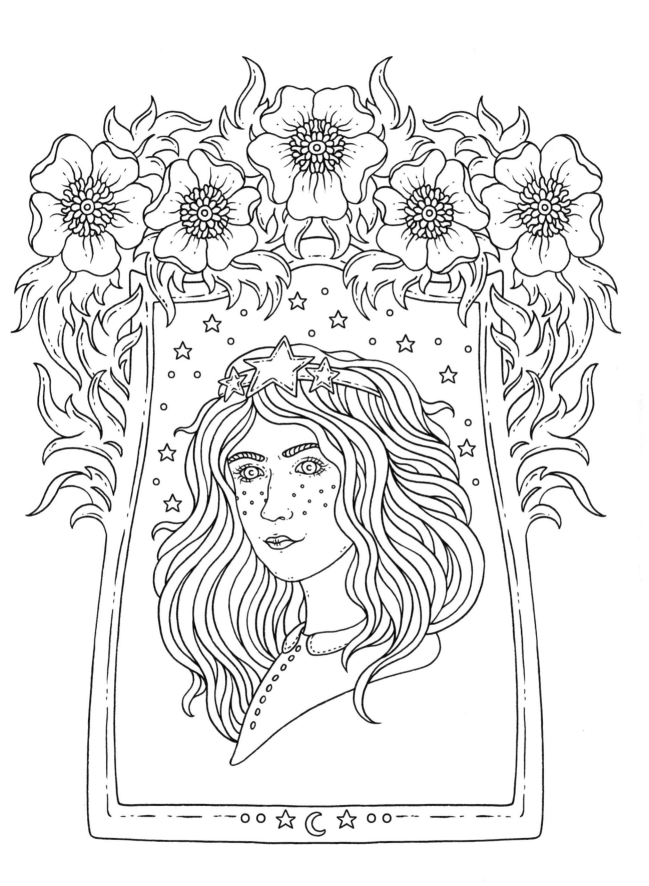

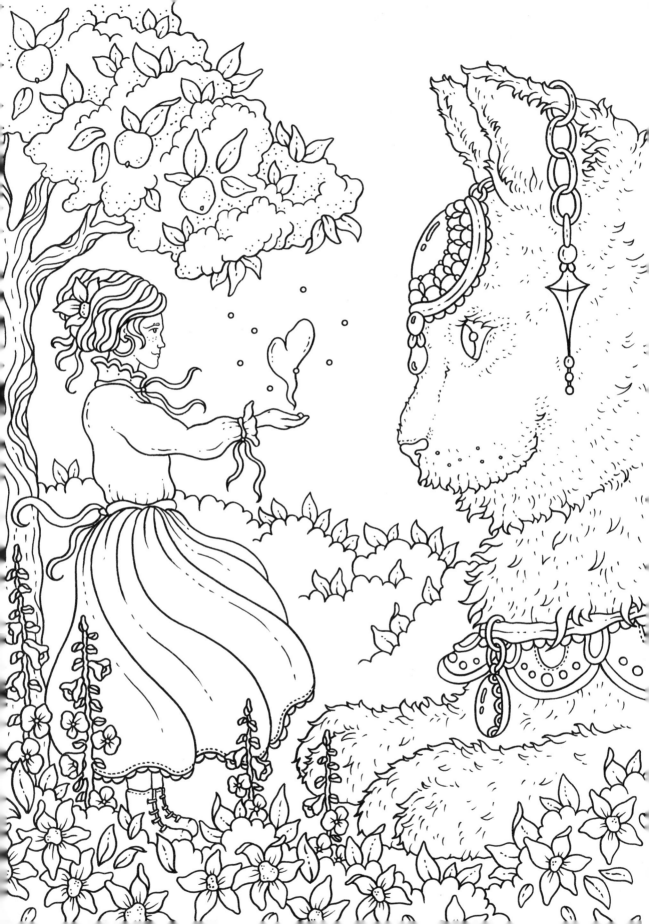

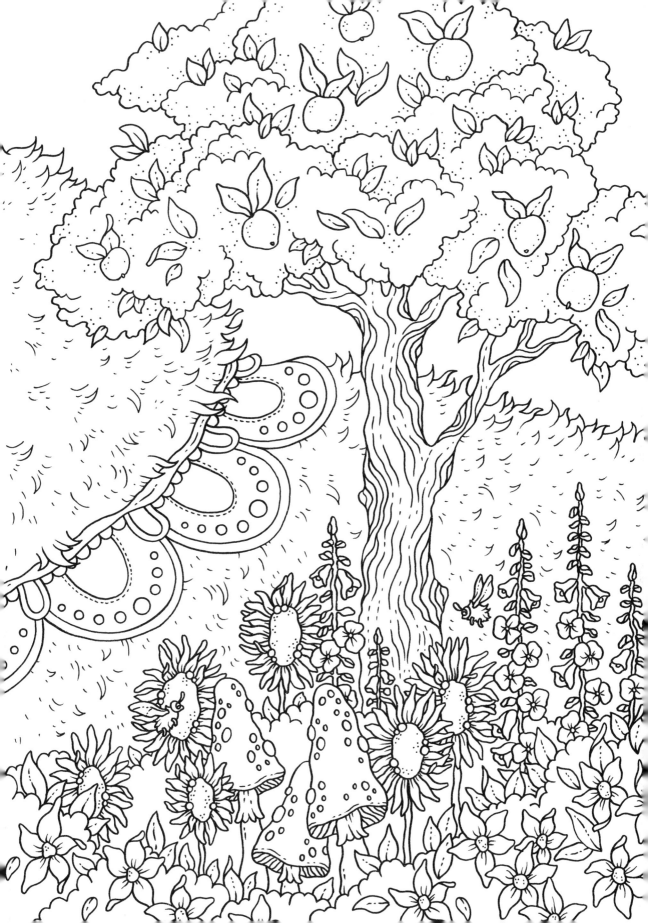

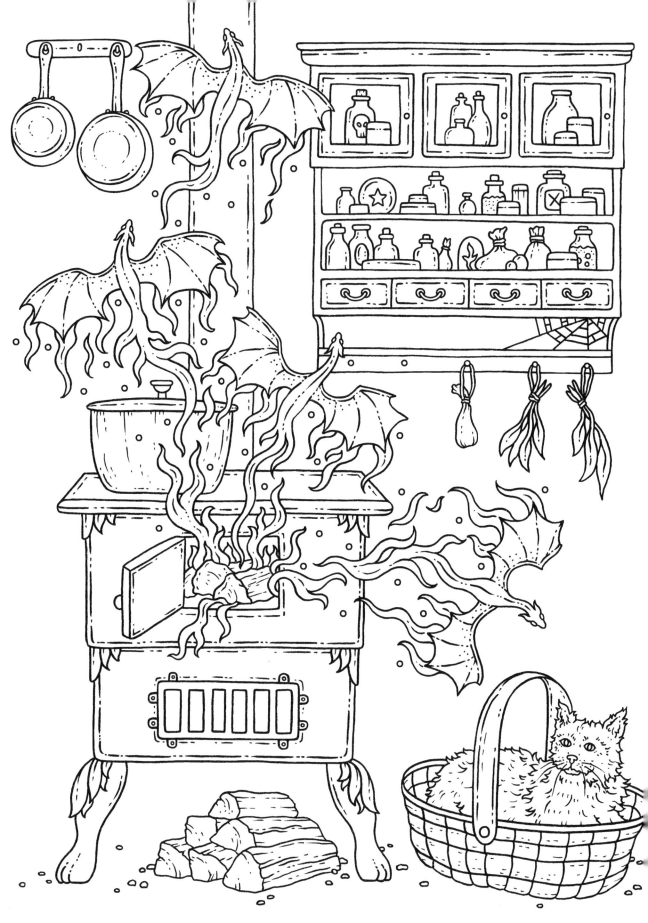

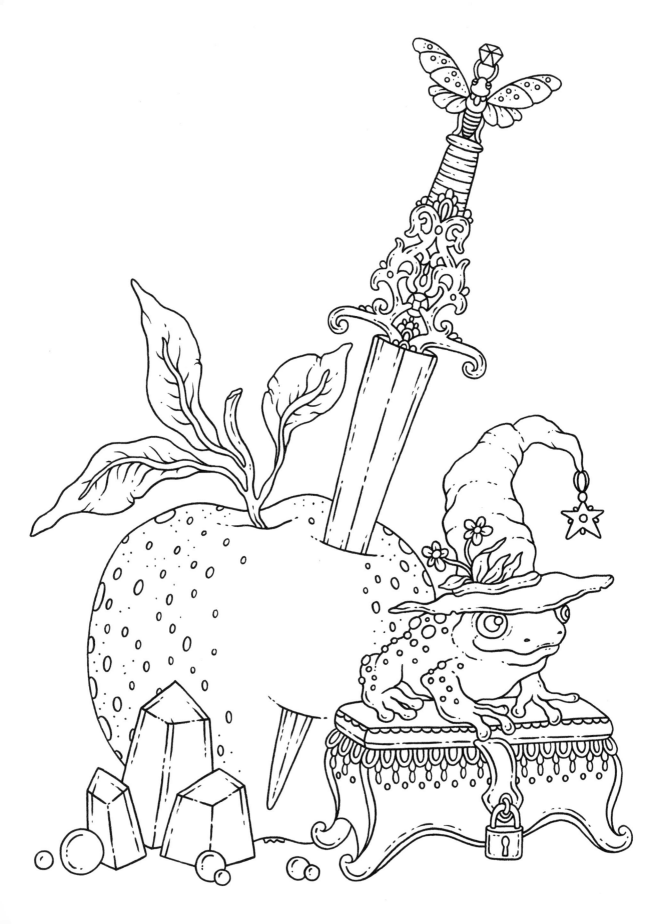

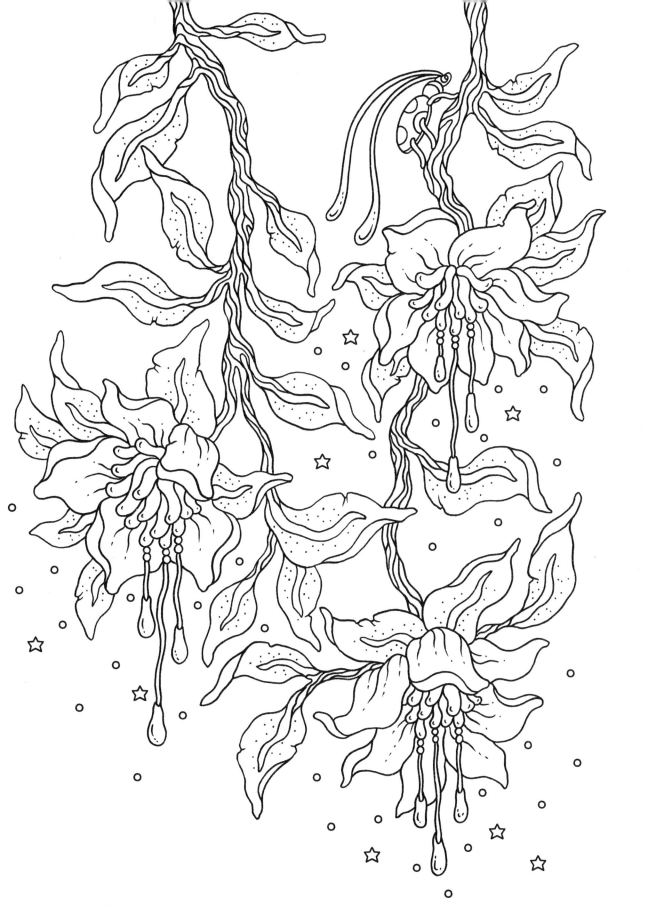

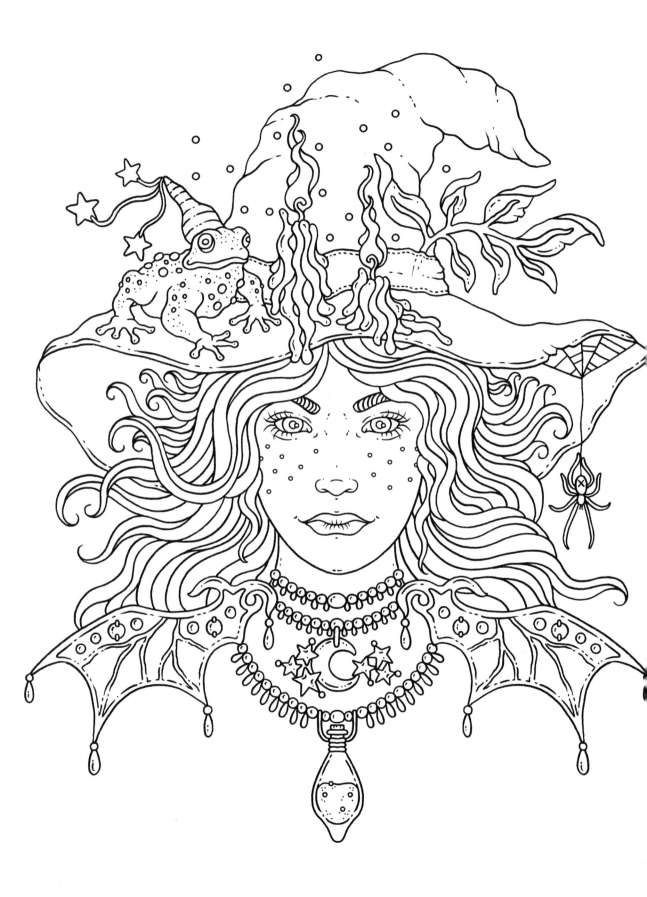

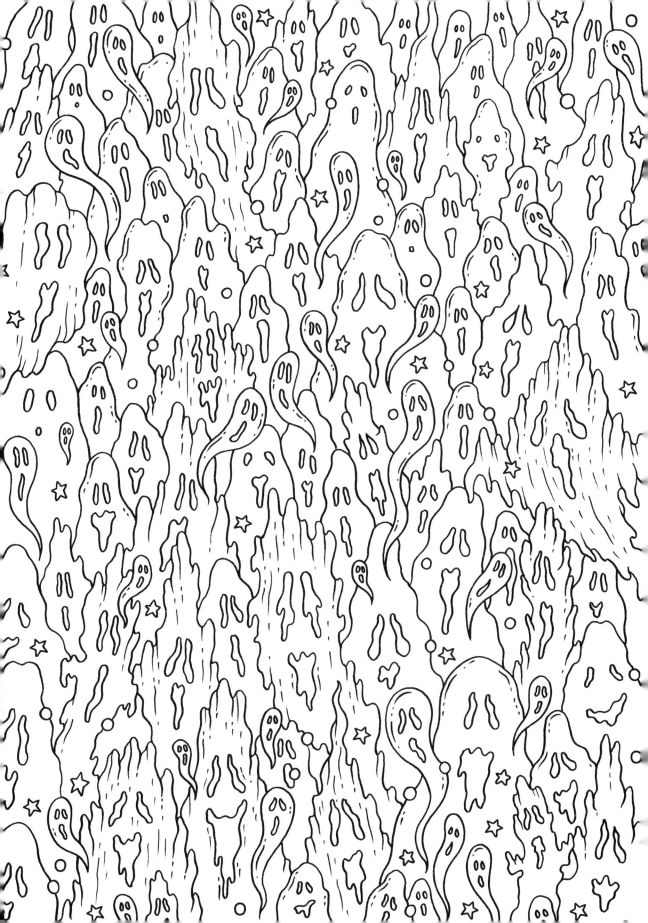

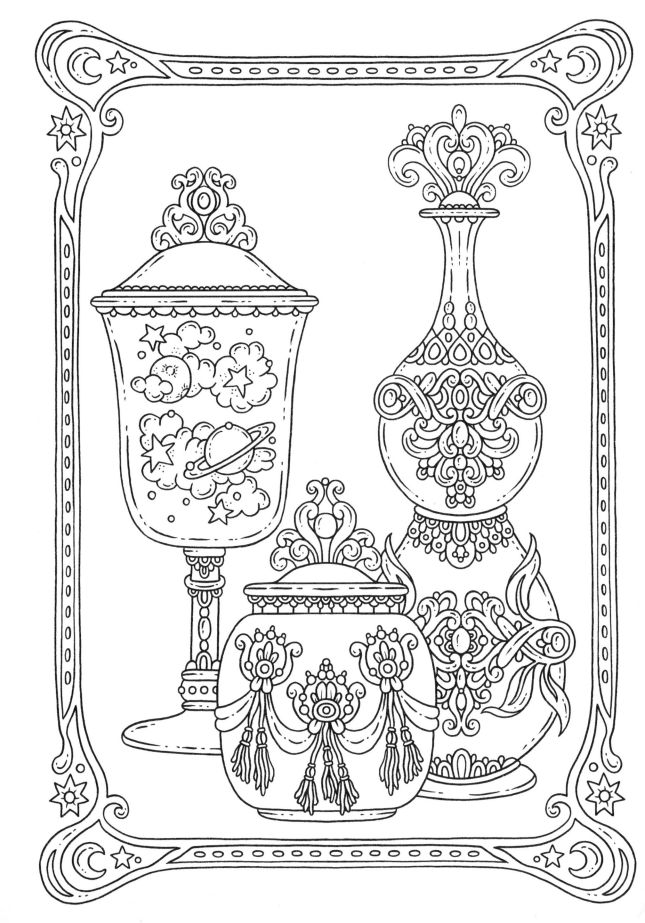

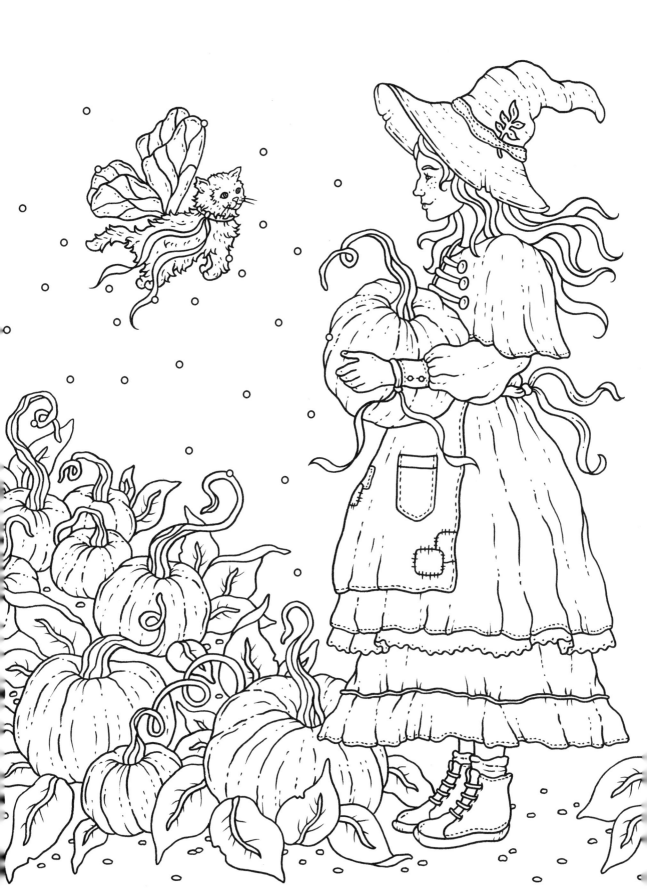

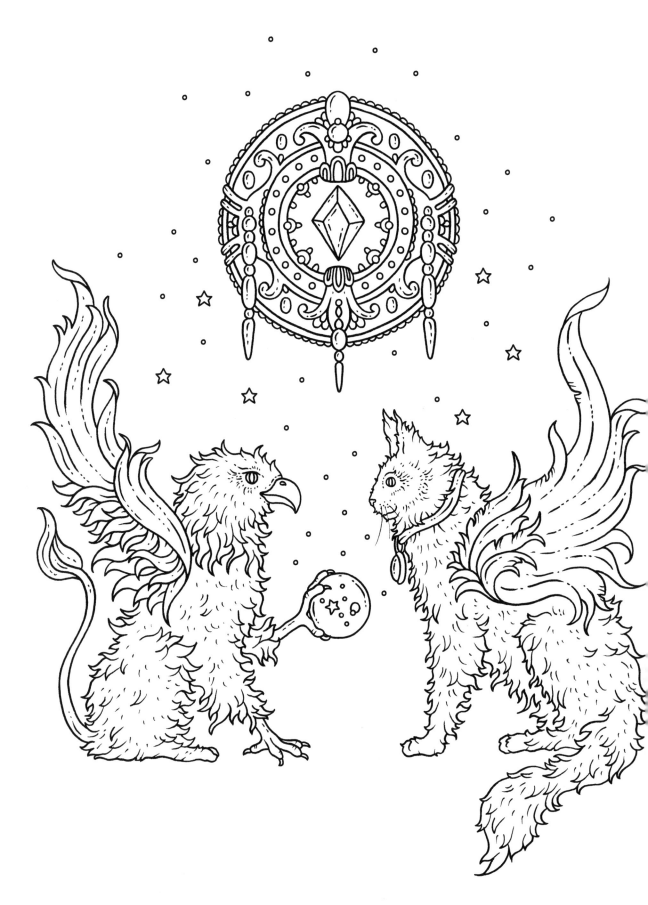

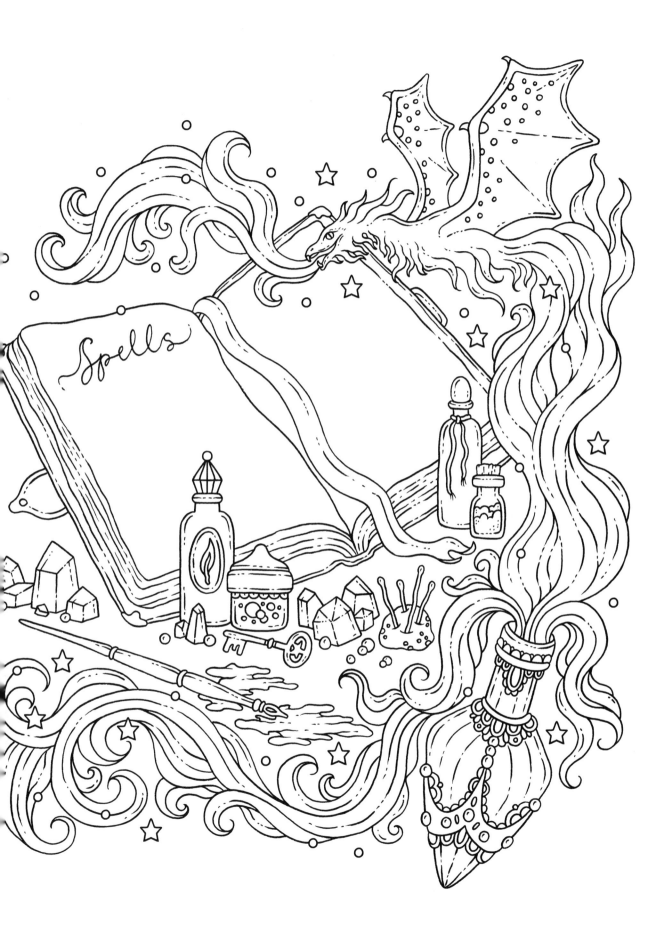

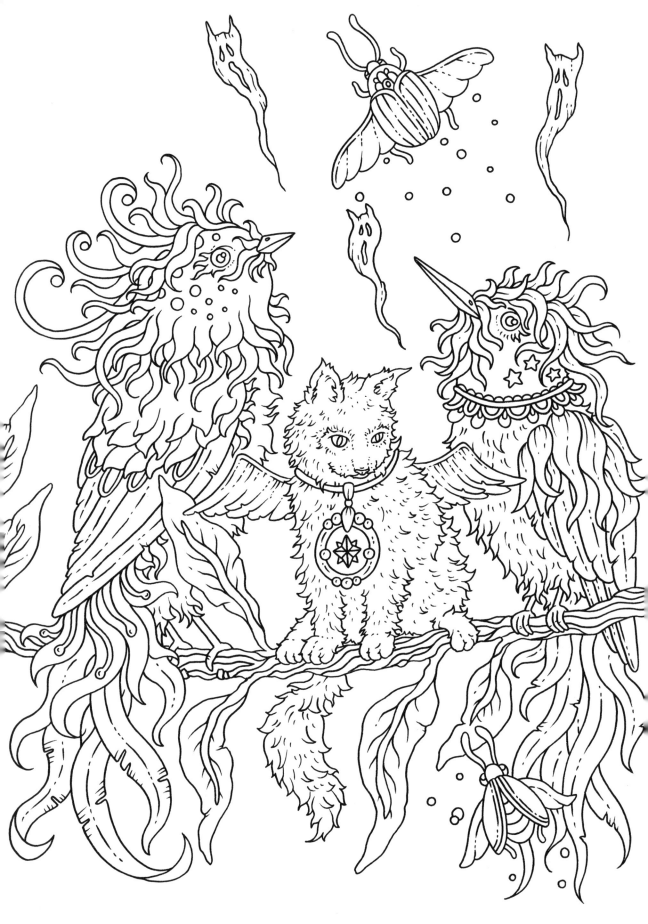

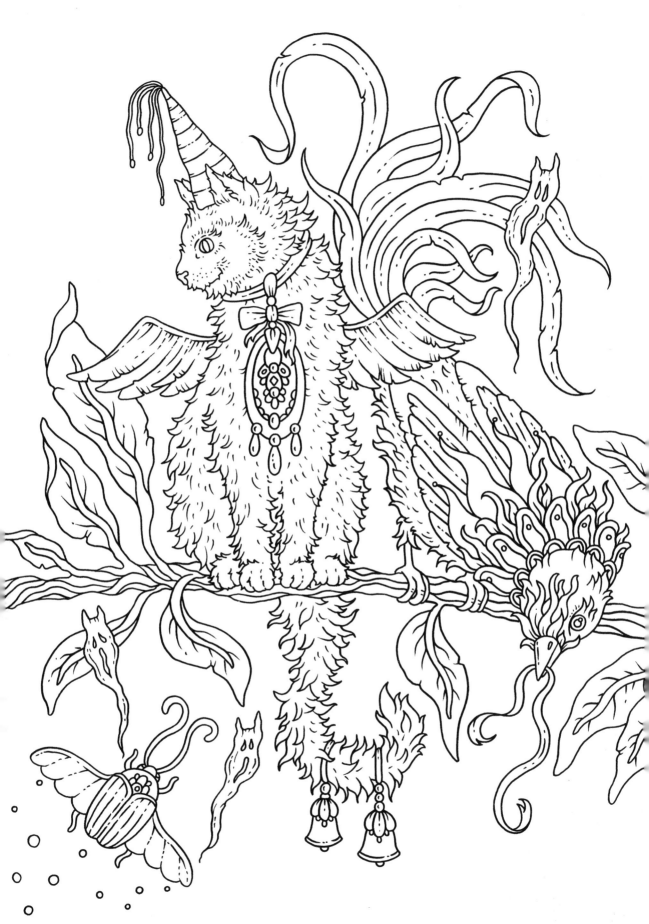

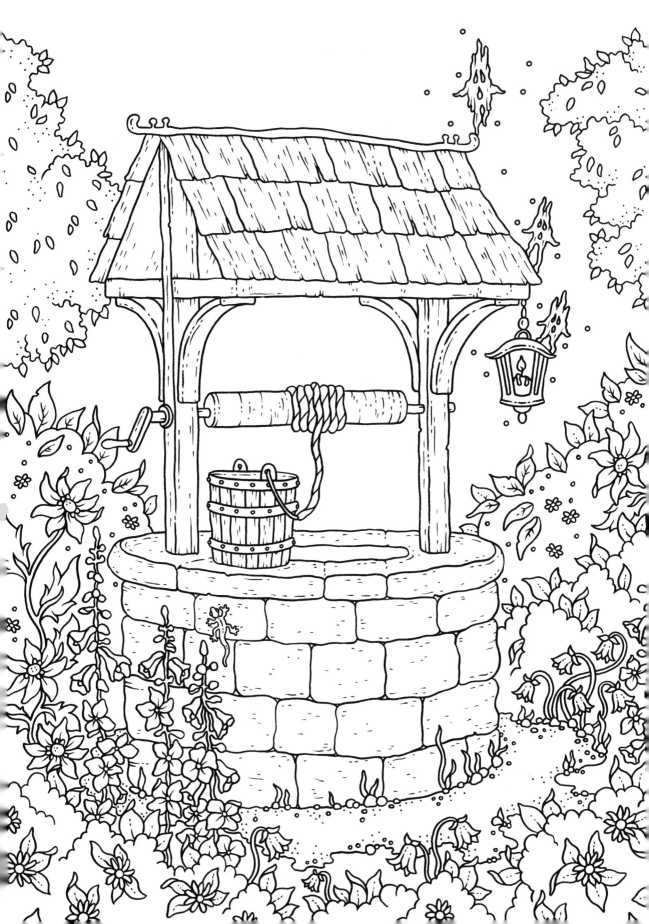

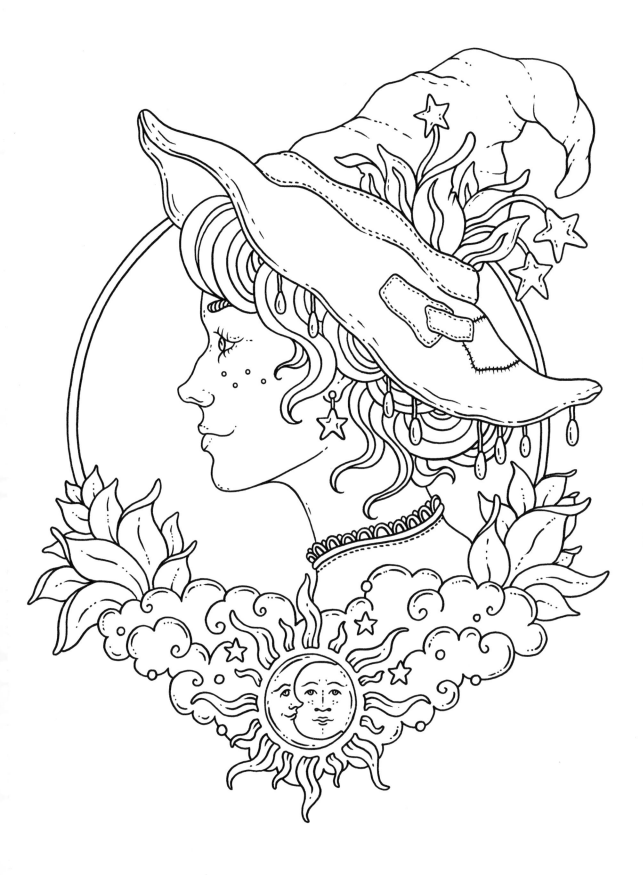

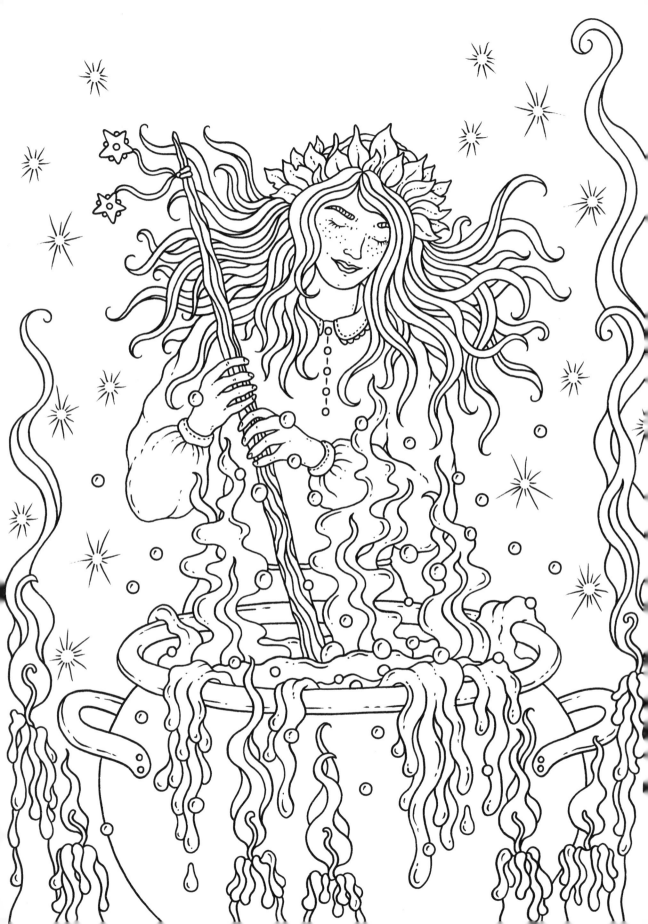

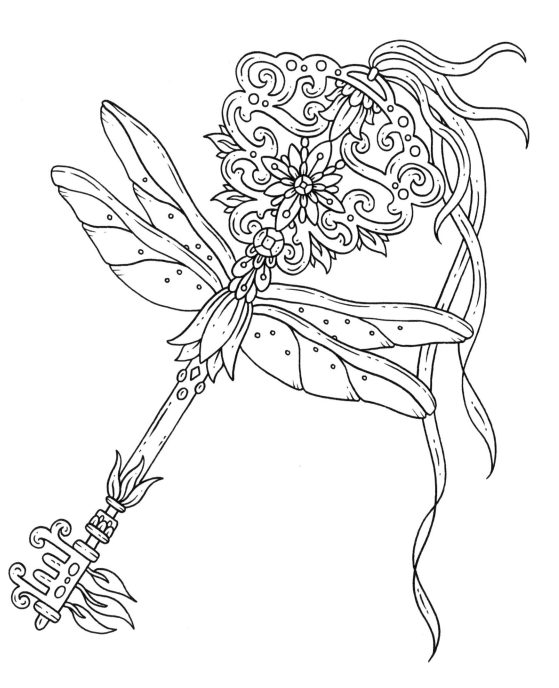

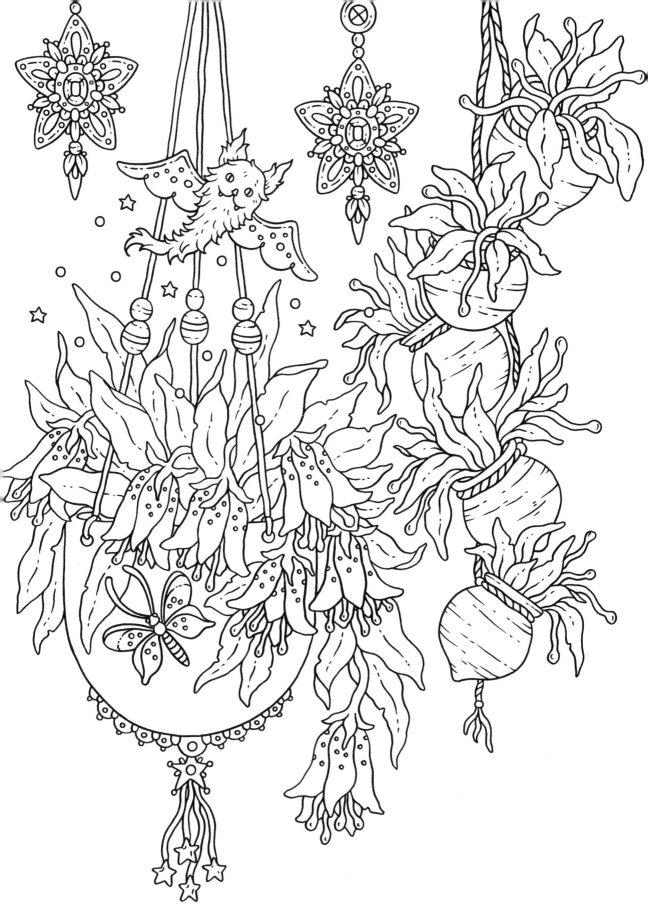

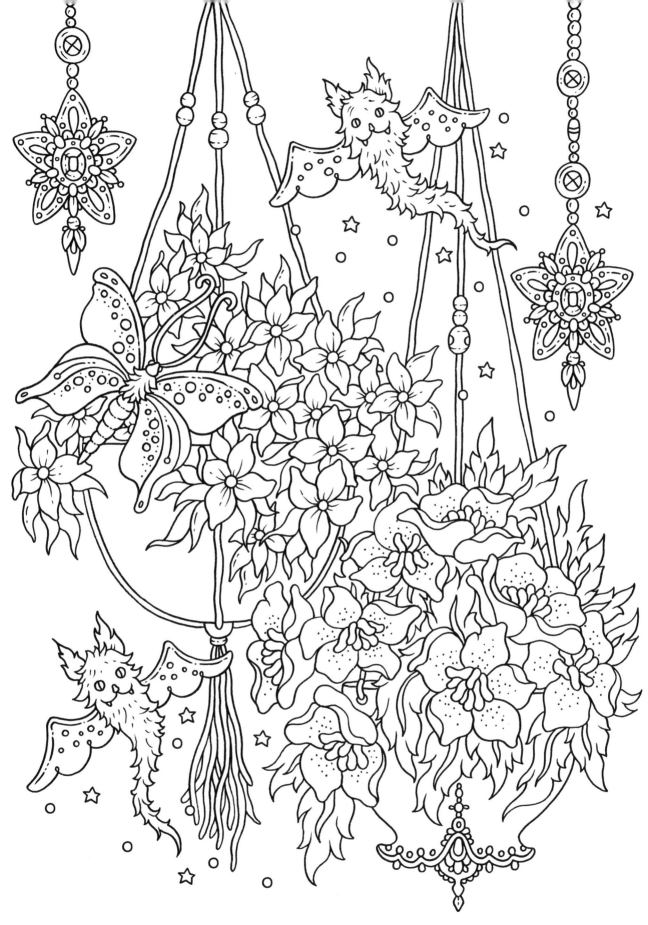

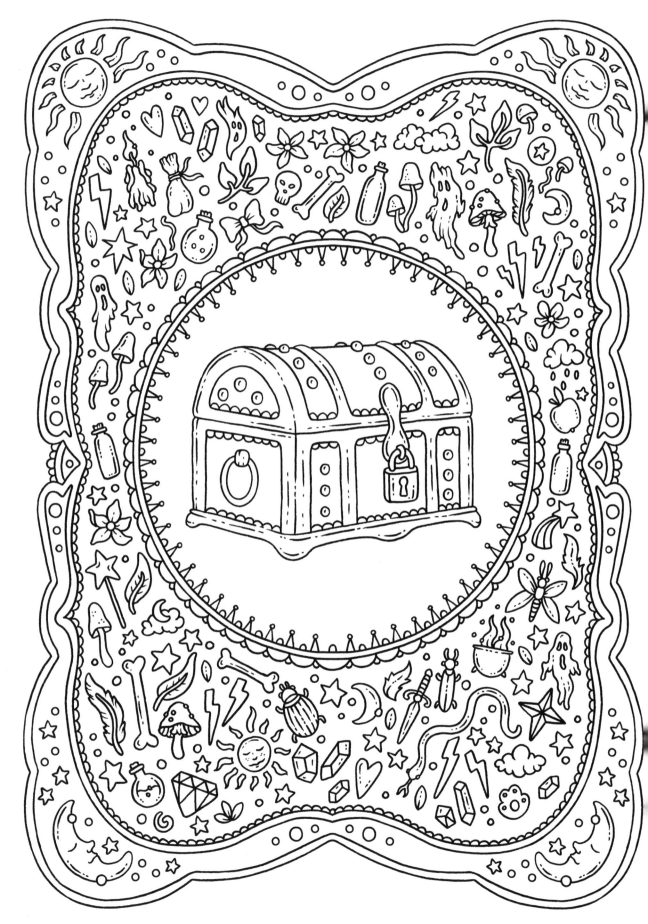

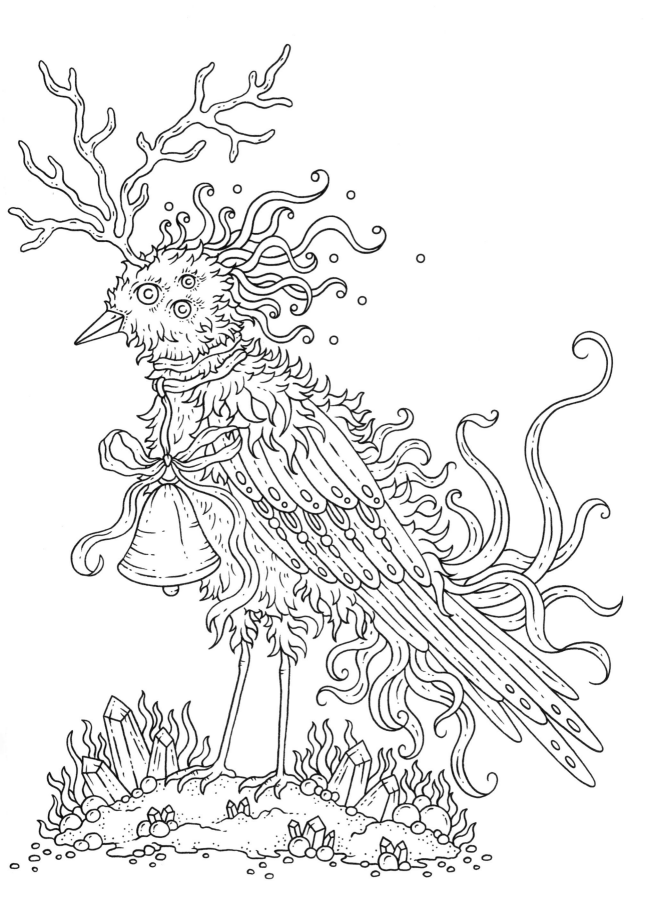

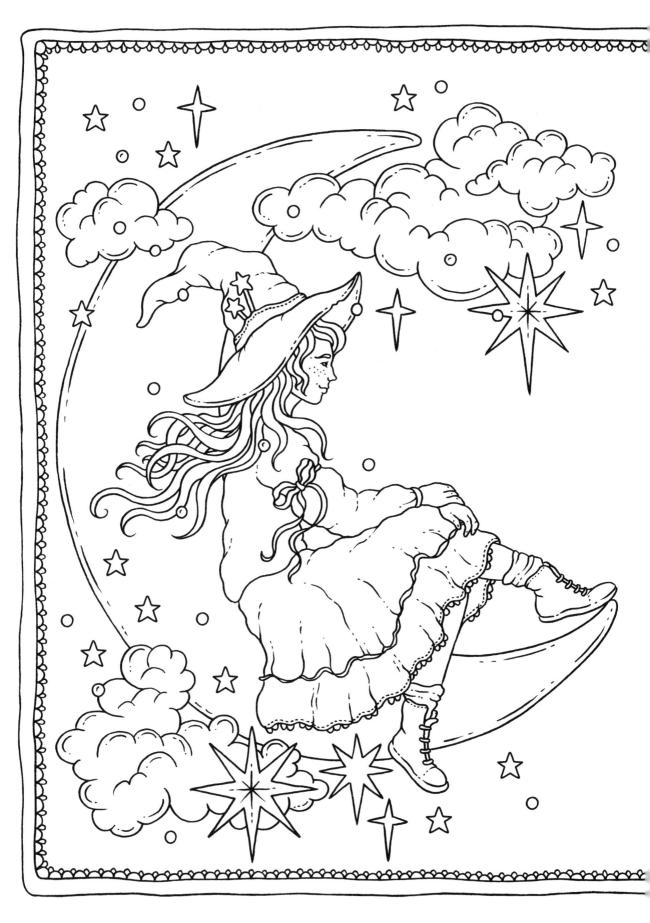

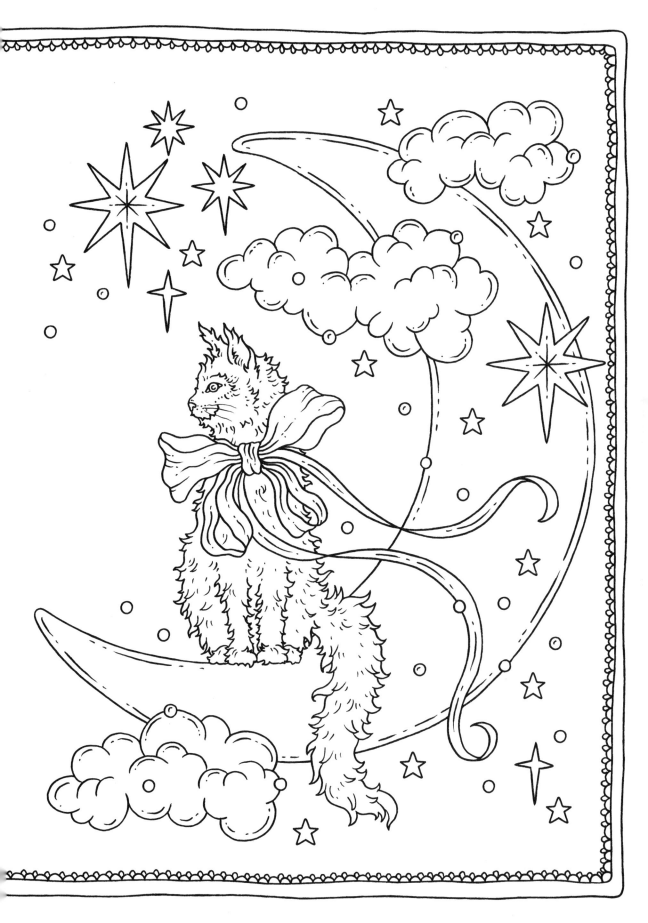

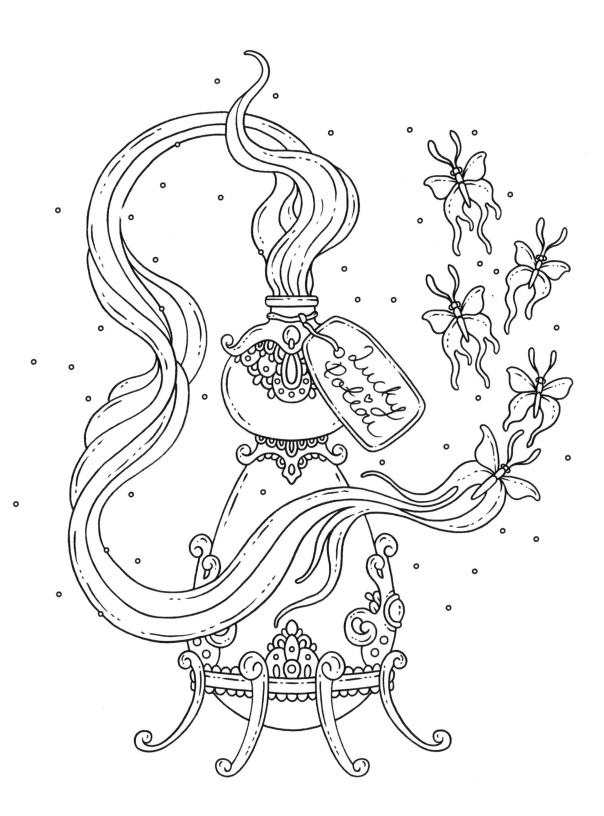